Little White Lies

Books by Beverly Lewis

GIRLS ONLY (GO!)
Youth Fiction

Dreams on Ice   Follow the Dream
Only the Best   Better Than Best
A Perfect Match   Photo Perfect
Reach for the Stars   Star Status

SUMMERHILL SECRETS
Youth Fiction

Whispers Down the Lane   House of Secrets
Secret in the Willows   Echoes in the Wind
Catch a Falling Star   Hide Behind the Moon
Night of the Fireflies   Windows on the Hill
A Cry in the Dark   Shadows Beyond the Gate

HOLLY'S HEART
Youth Fiction

Best Friend, Worst Enemy   Second-Best Friend
Secret Summer Dreams   Good-Bye, Dressel Hills
Sealed With a Kiss   Straight-A Teacher
The Trouble With Weddings   No Guys Pact
California Crazy   Little White Lies

www.BeverlyLewis.com

Little White Lies

Beverly Lewis

$BETHANYHOUSE
Minneapolis, Minnesota

Little White Lies
Copyright © 2003
Beverly Lewis

Cover illustration by Paul Casale
Cover design by Cheryl Neisen/Melinda Schumacher

Published by Bethany House Publishers
A Ministry of Bethany Fellowship International
11400 Hampshire Avenue South
Bloomington, Minnesota 55438
www.bethanyhouse.com

Printed in the United States of America by
Bethany Press International, Bloomington, Minnesota 55438

Library of Congress Cataloging-in-Publication Data

Lewis, Beverly
    Little white lies / by Beverly Lewis.

CIP applied for

ISBN 0-7642-2617-7

2002152465

Author's Note

Thanks to each reader who sent email or snail mail letters and school pix. Many of you are budding authors, and I encourage you to continue writing poetry, short stories, and novels. And do save everything you write. Someday your kids will be glad you did.

I simply could not write as many books as I do without help from my husband, Dave, and our young adult "kids." They bring me sandwiches, popcorn, and lots of hugs and kisses, especially when I'm on one of my "writing marathons." Four cheers to my dearest fans—they deserve oodles of credit!

Other loyal fans include my ultra-cool kid consultants who keep coming up with ingenious ideas—Janie, Amy, Julie, Shanna, Mindie, Jon, and Kirsten.

Special thanks to Kathy Torley, who answered my medical questions about angioplasty, and to Janet Turner, my travel agent, who helped answer airport security questions.

1

"Please say it's not true," Andrea Martinez said, pedaling hard to keep up with my bike. "You're going to California *again?*"

I nodded, amused. "It's not like you didn't sorta figure this, right?"

She didn't say a word.

Side by side, we rode our bikes down the tree-lined street in total silence. I stared straight ahead, letting the soothing summer breeze ripple the length of my hair.

I didn't have to glance at Andie to know she was fuming. Shoot, I could *feel* the frustration oozing out of her. When Andie didn't get her way, she often behaved like this, and I braced myself for the fierce argument that was sure to come.

Two weeks without her best friend wasn't exactly Andie's idea of summer fun. In fact, by the gray cloud on her face, it looked like she was going to have herself a full-blown pouting party. Just when I thought she might've grown up a little. After all, we *were* headed for our freshman year next fall. Besides that, we'd had the same ridiculous conversation last summer.

"Look, Andie," I said, trying to be kind, "just because I want to visit my dad doesn't mean I enjoy leaving you behind. You should know that by now."

There. Maybe that would calm her down.

Andie kept pedaling, standing up now as she worked her short legs. "All the coolest things happen in July around here, Holly," she insisted, slightly out of breath.

Whoa! Had she already forgotten our fabulous time at Camp Ouray? And what about that zany no-guys pact we'd concocted?

"So . . . church camp wasn't all that cool, then?" I asked sarcastically.

"That was *last* month," she shot back.

"Well, it's not like we haven't spent time together this summer," I pointed out. We coasted down a hill.

"Aw, c'mon," she argued. "Please stay in Dressel Hills. We'll have so-o much fun."

I could see this conversation was going nowhere fast. "Hey, I have an idea." I turned the corner and headed toward Andie's driveway. "Let's pretend we're having fun right now." I couldn't stop a mischievous smile from spreading across my face.

We parked our bikes on the front lawn. Andie cast a furtive glance my way. "Holly Meredith, you're completely hopeless." And with that she dashed into the house, calling to let her mom know she was home.

Completely hopeless?

I situated myself on Andie's front steps. Completely hopeless fell into an entirely different category from the simple teasing I'd just dished out. Completely hopeless had more to do with obnoxious little sisters like mine—Carrie, who was nine, and Stephanie, my stepsister, who was seven, going on infancy. Without the two of them forever sneaking around, my life might seem perfect right now.

Last week I'd squelched my excitement when Mom informed me that she didn't think Carrie would be going to California this time. "You know how close Carrie and

Stephie have become," she explained.

"Sure, Mom," I said, absolutely delighted.

When Uncle Jack came home for lunch, Mom asked his opinion. It only took a split second of whining from Stephie—telling how *horribly* lonely she'd be without Carrie—to bring Uncle Jack to his decision.

So it was settled. Carrie could skip the summer visit if it was okay with Daddy. And Mom lost no time phoning him in California. She escaped with the cordless phone into the living room while Carrie and I cleaned up the kitchen. I tried to listen in on Mom's end of the conversation, but it was difficult with all the kitchen clatter. As it turned out, Daddy had no problem with Carrie staying put here.

I was secretly thrilled. Daddy and I would have more time to spend together. At least this way, Carrie wouldn't jabber away every single second of our visit.

❤   ❤   ❤

I leaned back against the warm steps leading to Andie's front door and closed my eyes. Cheerful birds chirped around me everywhere. It was summer all right. One of the best times of year in Colorado. The heat from the porch steps radiated through my white shorts, so I stood up, letting the sun's rays warm my face instead.

"Thirsty?"

I twirled around. There stood Andie holding out a tall glass of lemonade. "Mmm, looks good. Thanks." I reached for the icy glass.

Andie shot me a hesitant look. "Are you totally sure about going off to California in just four days?"

"I don't have second thoughts if that's what you mean."

Her big brown eyes did that little rolling number. "Hey,

can't a girl ask a simple question?"

I was silent. She was pushing way too hard.

"If I could, I'd try and talk you out of it, you know." Andie took a long drink of lemonade, then looked up. "C'mon, let's go around to the backyard."

I followed her through the side yard toward the back of the house. Andie didn't wait for me to catch up. She kept twisting one of her dark curls around her finger, which *always* spells trouble. She was acting downright weird, like she had some big secret or something.

Around the back, positioned near several small aspen trees, a large jungle gym stretched out across one end of the yard. The play set had been purchased earlier this summer for Andie's three-year-old twin brothers, Jon and Chris. Numerous times, Andie and I had entertained the busy little boys while their parents were away. For pay, of course.

I went to the swings and sat down, swaying gently as I sipped my lemonade. Andie plopped down on the bottom of the slide.

"Look out—it might be hot!" I said, just as she scooted off and fell into the sand.

Getting up, she brushed off her cutoffs. "We oughta go swimming. You can get in on my Y membership." She sat on the swing next to me. "Want to?" she asked.

It *was* hot; a cool dip would feel fabulous. "Sure," I said. But Andie seemed suddenly distant—preoccupied—as she drank the rest of her lemonade. Was she brooding about the California thing?

I chewed on the ice at the bottom of my glass. "Something bugging you?" I asked.

"Sorta," she said softly.

"So talk to me."

She shuffled her feet around in the sand a bit before she spoke. "It's just that . . . I, oh, I don't know."

It wasn't like Andie to stall. If something was on her

mind, she never hesitated getting it out in the open. Especially with me. Andie and I had been close friends since preschool days.

"What *is* it?" I asked, my curiosity getting the best of me.

The sun glistened on Andie's hair, and she studied me with a clear, steady gaze. "What would you think if I went along with you?" She seemed almost shy. For the first time in her life.

"Let me get this straight," I said, smiling. "*You* want to go to California?"

"Yep. With you," she emphasized.

"Sounds like a good idea to me, but what about your parents? Do you think they'll agree?"

Her smile faded quickly. "I don't know. My parents are real protective."

"Well, why would you want to go in the first place?" I asked, eager to get to the bottom of this.

"It's just that I never get to go *anywhere*," she exaggerated. "I was born here, and except for camping, we hardly ever leave Dressel Hills." She stood up just then and flung her arms wide. Something like the way Maria does in the opening scene to *The Sound of Music*. "There's a world out there just waiting for me. I don't want to stagnate and die here in Colorado."

I giggled. Now, *this* was the Andie I knew and loved. And high drama at its best.

"Okay, okay, I get the picture. But don't forget our choir tour to California, and there was the Grand Canyon, and—"

She grabbed the chain on my swing. "So you'll take me along?" she begged, her face inches from mine. I could smell the lemon on her breath.

"It's not up to me to decide," I said more seriously. "Even if it's okay with your folks, I'll still have to clear it with my dad and stepmom." Then I remembered Jon and Chris. "Who's going to help with your brothers while you're gone?"

"Two weeks?" She waved her hand like she was swatting flies. "No problem."

"So you think your mom can manage?"

"I guess we'll just have to ask." She motioned for me to go with her into the house.

"Wait." I stopped at the back door. "Maybe we should talk this over with my dad first, uh, you know, since he hasn't seen you for a while."

Andie's countenance dimmed. "Oh, yeah. Maybe he won't want his daughter bringing home her *Hispanic* friend."

I stared at her, shocked. "What's that supposed to mean?"

She put her hands on her hips. "So . . . he doesn't care that I'm Hispanic, does he?"

"Look, Andie, I don't know what you're getting at, but Daddy's not prejudiced. Not even close. Besides, he's a Christian now."

Her voice quivered. "I know. But I've heard how it is in some places for different ethnic groups—even worse than in a small town like Dressel Hills."

I reached for Andie and gave her a hug. "You're my friend. Nothing will ever change that."

Andie started to tremble.

"Andie?"

Quickly, she wiped her eyes, pulling away.

"What's wrong?" I whispered. "Are you all right?"

She shook her head, eyes filling with tears.

"Has someone said something?"

"I don't want to talk about it," she managed to say. "Maybe we should just forget the whole dumb idea." She turned away quickly so I couldn't see her cry. "I'll see you later, Holly."

"No, wait," I called to her. But it was too late. Andie had gone inside. She closed the door without even the slightest glance back.

Tears stung my eyes as I thought of someone, anyone,

insulting my friend. How rotten!

It was obvious Andie wanted to be left alone. As much as I hated leaving her like this, I knew it would do absolutely no good to ring the doorbell, hoping she'd answer. Andie was too hurt to talk.

She and I were opposites in that way. If I was hurting, I wanted someone around. Someone who would talk to me and help me through my tunnel of pain. Andie and my mom were both good about pursuing me at times like that. Even when I might insist that I wanted to be alone, they knew deep down I really didn't.

Feelings of concern pricked at me as I got on my bike. Andie had actually become hostile, and all it took was a single comment about Daddy not having seen her lately. She'd mistaken my words completely—jumped to conclusions.

Something, or *someone*, was bugging her. Why, I didn't know. But I was determined to find out.

2

When I arrived home, supper was almost ready to be served.

I sniffed the air as I came into the kitchen. Oven-baked chicken, yum. "Smells like the Fourth of July all over again," I said.

"Oh, there you are, Holly-Heart." Mom gave me a quick hug. "Hungry?"

"Starved."

"Well, good," she said, turning around to check on the oven. "I didn't make thirty pieces of chicken for nothing, did I?"

"Thirty?"

Some quick math told me that with six kids, plus Mom and Uncle Jack, there were eight of us. Divided into thirty, that's about four pieces each. "Why so many?" I asked, even more puzzled when I spied two huge steaming bowls of mashed potatoes.

"Well," she said, a twinkle in her eye, "we're having company."

"We are?"

"Stan has a new friend." She reached for two potholders and opened the oven door. Tantalizing smells escaped and wafted their way through the kitchen.

"A girl?" I asked, hoping not—for Andie's sake.

"No girl," Mom said. She carried a huge oven tray over to the island bar and began to place pieces of chicken on a large platter.

"Who, then?" I checked to see if the dining room table was set. It was.

"Oh, just a guy he met down at the Y," Mom said. "I'm sure you'll find him interesting."

"What's that supposed to mean? You're not setting me up with . . ."

"Oh, Holly, you know how I feel about girl-boy stuff at your age." She untied her apron and flung it over the drain board near the sink. "Can't I say something nice about a boy without you getting defensive?"

"Sorry, Mom, I just—"

"Just what?" It was Carrie. My little sister had materialized out of thin air.

"Carrie," Mom reprimanded. "How many times have I told you not to do that?"

I sighed. "Oh, give or take two thousand."

"That's *not* true!" Carrie shouted, shooting daggers at me with her beady eyes.

"You mean you haven't been getting A-pluses in sneaking up on people? Tell me it isn't so," I sneered.

"Girls, girls," Mom said, wagging her finger in front of our faces. "Be sweet to each other. You only have a few more days together before Holly leaves for California."

"Yes," Carrie whispered, flicking her long ponytail.

I didn't say what *I* was thinking. It wouldn't have pleased the Lord. Mom either.

"So," Carrie inquired, "who's coming for dinner?"

"Never mind," I said, turning her around and giving her a gentle shove.

Mom smiled. "You'll both find out soon enough."

Carrie turned around and wrinkled her nose at me.

"Holly, will you pour the iced tea, please?" Mom asked.

Gladly. Anything to get away from my pesky sister.

♥　♥　♥

When everything was in its place on the table, Mom rang her Precious Moments dinner bell. Mark, Phil, and Stephie came running up the family room steps. Stan and his friend came barreling up next. I wondered why Stan avoided my eyes as he walked through the kitchen.

Funny. Just when things were perking along on an even keel with my fairly snooty stepbrother, a thing like bringing a friend home for supper threw everything out of whack. How could that be?

I studied Stan's friend discreetly. Medium frame . . . not quite as tall as Stan. Average brown hair, sort of mousy, actually. And horror of horrors—a ripe pimple. Right next to his nose!

Uncle Jack waited for us to get situated at the table before he offered the blessing. Afterward, he turned to Stan, who sat across from me, and asked him to introduce his friend.

"Sure, Dad," Stan began. "Everyone," and here he made eye contact with each of us at the table, even me, "this is Ryan Davis, one of the guys on the swim team at the Y."

Stan introduced each of us individually, starting with Stephie, the youngest. When he came to me, he said, "Ryan's into creative writing . . . like you, Holly." He paused. "Maybe you could show him that story you got published last year." He smiled like he was actually proud of my accomplishment.

"Really?" Ryan said, his hazel eyes lighting up. "Published?" He said it like it was a sacred act or something. "What magazine?"

"I'll show you after supper," I said, not really caring about this little charade Stan was playing. Using me to impress his pimply-faced friend.

"Okay," Ryan said, smiling too broadly for my taste.

Mom and Uncle Jack carried the conversation with Ryan and Stan clear through dessert. Now and then I caught snatches of Carrie and Stephie whispering next to me. Sounded like they were making plans for the two weeks I'd be gone. I grinned. What a fabulous break from these two—escaping to Daddy's wonderful beach house overlooking the ocean, relaxing in the sun, sipping iced tea. Ah, what a way to spend fourteen carefree days. No time pressure. No stress. I could scarcely wait.

I was daydreaming, blocking out Stan and Ryan's jibber-jabber, when suddenly I heard Andie's name mentioned. I spooned up some of Mom's apple crisp and a scoop of ice cream on the side, trying to act disinterested. Staring at my plate, I chewed in silence, but I was all ears.

Stan was saying he and Ryan had bumped into Andie at the Y yesterday. "We were going in and she was ready to leave," he said nonchalantly.

I waited for him to mention that Andie was his girlfriend and that they'd been going out off and on. But he was silent about that.

Strange.

Mom wiped her mouth with a napkin, then reached over and touched my left hand. "I think Holly and Andie must have the longest-running friendship around Dressel Hills," she said. "Right, honey?"

I nodded.

Uncle Jack nodded, too. "I'd say they're nearly sisters."

A smirk swept across Ryan's face. "Well, they sure don't look it." He snickered.

"Very funny," I replied.

"Well . . . you know," Ryan muttered.

"No, I don't," I said. "And I think you'd better spell it out."

Stan frowned, casting his stern gaze on me. "Just drop it," he said.

"Look," I said, directing my comment to Stan, "Andie's fabulous and *you*, of all people, should know that."

He didn't comment, and it infuriated me. Why wasn't he sticking up for Andie? I didn't get it.

I slid my chair away from the table, remembering the way Andie had cried earlier. "Excuse me, please."

"Holly!" Mom said stiffly.

Ignoring her, I ran to the kitchen and grabbed the portable phone.

"What's your problem?" Stan said as I flew through the dining room.

Turning around, I stared him down. "Think about it," I said in my coldest voice. "Andie was perfectly fine for you"— I forced my gaze away from him and looked at Ryan—"until now."

The entire family was staring at me. I could almost hear the wheels in Mom's brain turning. *What's gotten into her?* she was probably thinking.

Sure as shootin', Uncle Jack was thinking something along the same lines, except his face was less revealing. He leaned back, scratched his chin, and winked in a fatherly fashion—to let me know he'd have a talk with Stan later, no doubt. It was just what I needed, even though Uncle Jack was only my stepdad—the best around.

Ryan's voice rose out of the silence. "Very nice meeting you, Holly."

I wanted to say "Go pop your pimple," but I turned and fled to my room. I choked back the horrible thought, only to have it rise up like a flood: *Had Stan's friend ridiculed Andie to her face?*

I closed my bedroom door behind me. My hand shook as I gripped the portable phone. It was time to get to the bottom of things.

3

The phone rang a zillion times. C'mon, Andie, pick up, I thought.

Two more rings.

Where is she? I wondered.

Frazzled, I let the phone continue to ring.

At last, someone answered. It was Andie's father. "Martinez residence," he said.

"Is Andie there?" I asked hesitantly.

"Oh, hello, Holly." He paused. "Uh, I believe she is, but I think she's in her room. May I take a message?"

I switched the phone to my left ear. "Is . . . is Andie all right?"

"Well, I don't know that she's ill if that's what you mean." He cleared his throat.

I figured he didn't know what I was talking about.

"Okay, well, just tell her I called, and she can call me back whenever."

"I will certainly tell her."

We said good-bye and hung up.

This wasn't working. I *had* to talk to Andie!

I figured I'd better wait awhile before leaving to go visit her. The way I felt right now, it wouldn't be smart to go dashing downstairs. I didn't trust my feelings toward Stan or his disgusting friend.

Why had they talked that way about Andie, anyway?

My cat leaped up onto my window seat, as though he were inviting me to join him. So I did. There, on the padded pillows, I snuggled with Goofey, letting the rumble of his purring comfort me. More than anything, I wished I could talk to Andie. Maybe she didn't need me to help her through whatever was bugging her, but I needed her—to find out if what I suspected was true.

To keep from freaking out, I began to pray. "Dear Lord, I don't know what's going on between Stan and Andie, but you do." I paused, hesitating to pray about Ryan Davis. What a jerk!

I took a deep breath, then continued my prayer. "Uh . . . Stan's friend, you know him, his name's Ryan. Well, I don't think he's the best kind of friend for Stan, but then, you know all things, so I'll let it go with that, Lord. Amen."

It was the most pathetic prayer I'd ever prayed.

I glanced at my watch. Almost seven o'clock. I got up and gently laid Goofey down on my window seat. Then I opened my bedroom door and leaned my head out, listening. Stan and Mom were talking in the kitchen. Closing my eyes, I tried to visualize the kitchen cleanup schedule.

Fairly certain that it wasn't my turn, I breathed a sigh of relief. Maybe, just maybe, I could slip out of the house without encountering Stan. Or Ryan. It was worth a try. Besides, my curiosity was propelling me over to Andie's. I had to know what was going on. She would easily clear things up for me if I could just get her to talk. One thing was sure—with Ryan hanging around over here, it would be next to impossible to get a straight answer out of Stan.

Quietly, I closed my door and tiptoed down the hall to the stairs. I made my way cautiously to the landing.

Carrie came racing through, nearly slamming into me.

"Holly," she said much too loudly, "I need your help."

"Not now," I whispered, looking around, hoping Stan and company weren't nearby.

Just then Stephie came in from the living room. "Ple-ease help Carrie and me," she begged. "It won't take long."

I glanced over my shoulder toward the kitchen. Too late. Stan had spotted me.

"Can't now." I pushed past the girls. "Maybe later." Heart pounding, I hurried toward the front door.

"Wait up!" Stan called after me.

I ignored him and kept going.

"Holly, would you wait?"

There was no looking back now. I hopped on my bike and sped away. When I was out of reach, I glanced back, surprised to see Stan sitting on the front steps, staring at the ground. Had he sensed where I was headed? And if so, what didn't he want me to find out?

Now I was *really* curious. If I could just get Andie to talk.

Three blocks away, still on Downhill Court—my street— I saw the Miller twins riding their bikes, heading west toward the main drag through our ski village resort.

"Hey, Holly," the girls called in unison. Funny how that worked with twins. Not only did they look alike, they thought alike, too.

"Hey," I said, riding up to them. "Where're you two headed?"

Kayla spoke up. "Footloose and Fancy Things is having a giant sale on their summer stock. Why don't you join us?"

"I'm almost broke," I said, which was true. I'd spent nearly all my summer baby-sitting money on a year's sponsorship for an overseas child.

"I'll be glad to loan you some money," Paula offered, smiling brightly.

"Thanks, anyway," I said. "I'm pretty well set with clothes for summer."

Paula moved her bike out of the street and onto the sidewalk. Kayla did, too. I stayed put, eager to get going. Unfortunately, it looked like the twins wanted to engage in small talk.

"I'm in a hurry," I said apologetically.

"Headed to Andie's?" Paula asked.

"Uh-huh." I said it casually, like it was no big deal.

Kayla flipped her shoulder-length brown hair. "How's she doing *today?*"

Before I could answer, Paula added, "We were really concerned about her emotional state yesterday at the Y."

The Y?

Quickly, I moved my bike out of the street and up onto the sidewalk beside Kayla's. "What happened at the Y?"

Kayla's eyes widened and her thick, mascara-laden lashes twittered. "Andie didn't tell you?"

"Not exactly."

Paula put the kickstand down on her bike and came over to me. Kayla too. Something was up. We were actually huddled.

Paula started filling in some important details. "Kayla and I had just arrived at the Y yesterday afternoon when we ran into Andie. She was crying as she came out."

I swallowed hard. "Crying?"

Kayla sighed. "It looked like she and Stan had gotten into it, or worse."

"Stan?" I echoed.

"He and some guy were standing inside the lobby," Kayla explained. "And Stan looked upset."

"Who was the other guy?" I asked.

Paula glanced at Kayla. "We'd never seen him around here before," she said.

"Not at church or school," Kayla added.

"It's possible that he's a high school student," Paula suggested. "He seemed a little older than Stan."

"What did he look like?" I asked.

Paula glanced up, like she was trying to pull a description out of the air. "I don't remember."

"I remember something," Kayla said with a giggle. "He had a very large pimple near his nose."

Paula nodded, laughing, too.

My pulse raced. "You're saying the guy with Stan had a pimple?"

Paula and Kayla stared at me. "Why?" Paula asked. "Do you know him?"

I exhaled. "Maybe."

"Well, whoever it was," Kayla said, "he sure was a master intimidator."

"Yeah," Paula piped up. "He was downright sarcastic."

Whew! Things were beginning to take shape.

Kayla draped her arm around her twin's shoulders. "The jerk made a comment about Paula's eyes—that they didn't match mine. And if we were really twins, one of us ought to wear a little more mascara."

I gasped. "He said *that?*"

Paula nodded. I could tell by her grin that she was rather proud that someone had noticed she'd opted for the more natural look.

"I tell you, the guy's outspoken," Kayla said.

"No kidding," I whispered. Man, it was anybody's guess what the guy had said to Andie about her being Hispanic!

♥   ♥   ♥

By the time I got to Andie's house it was almost eight o'clock. I could see the light in her bedroom upstairs as I rode my bike into the driveway. Walking around the side of the house, I stood under her open window and called up to her. "Andie, come to the window."

In a flash, her perky curls appeared at the window.

"What are you doing down there?" she asked, her brown eyes questioning my return.

"We have to talk," I said matter-of-factly.

"Now?"

"Can you come out?" I stepped back away from the house, trying to see her better. "Or should I come up?"

She frowned slightly. "Well, I guess I could. Meet me out front."

I hurried to the front of the two-story house, to the same steps I'd sat on earlier. Now they felt cool to the touch as I eased myself down onto the cement, waiting for my friend. It seemed strange that I'd be sitting here again, especially since I knew Andie needed some space from whatever had happened. But I needed to hear the story from her lips.

Crickets chirped noisily as Andie finally emerged from the front door. She was dressed in a plain red T-shirt. Her cutoffs were frayed around the edges, and she was barefooted. "What's the occasion?" she said as she sat down, a bottle of red nail polish in her hand.

How should I start? I wondered. I sure didn't want to put her through the same kind of pain she'd expressed earlier today.

"Hey, can't your best friend just show up for no reason?" I said. "I was worried about you." I put my arm around her shoulders.

"I'll survive."

"Of course you will. And I'm going to make sure you do." I removed my arm as she leaned over to paint her toenails.

I sat there, fidgeting with my fingers, studying my cuticles and pushing them back till I could see the round white moon shapes underneath. I wished for some sort of breakthrough.

Some way to open up the subject of Stan and Ryan without causing Andie additional pain.

"Have you thought any more about taking me to California with you?" she asked, still bending over, talking to her toes.

I hadn't had time to think about that. I'd been too busy worrying about her encounter with Stan to contemplate my trip to California. "It'd be fabulous" was all I said.

"What about your dad and stepmom?" She straightened up and dipped the brush into the polish. "Did you ask them?"

"They do have a huge house," I said. "Plenty of room for you. But what about your parents? Think they'd let you go with me?"

"Here's the deal," she said. "If you get the okay from your dad, I'll take it from there with my parents, okay?"

"Sure, that'll work."

She started polishing her toenails again. "You're flying out this Monday, right?"

"At 12:15," I said. "Think you can get up before noon?"

She laughed. "Yeah, right. Isn't summer terrific?"

I nodded. Summer made the whole rest of the year worth living. "Guess we'd better start planning things, or you might not get a seat on my flight. I'll call my dad tonight."

This conversation was going in a totally different direction than I'd intended. I wondered how to address the subject of what had happened yesterday at the Y. Then an idea popped into my head.

"So . . . does Stan know you want to go with me?" I asked.

She stared at me incredulously. "Stan who?"

I realized I'd opened up a fresh wound.

"He couldn't care less where I go or what I do," she announced to the approaching sunset. "I'm sorry to inform you, Holly, but your stepbrother is a despicable bigot."

I frowned. "Excuse me?" I needed more to go on than this impromptu indictment.

"And that friend of his . . ." She blew air out through her lips.

"What friend?" I quizzed her, almost sure she was talking about Ryan Davis.

"Oh, Ryan somebody." She waved her hand in front of her face. "You should've heard what he said to me."

Bingo. Just what I'd been waiting to hear!

4

"What did Ryan say?" I asked.

"Stan was in on it, too," Andie insisted. "He acted like he hardly knew me. Especially after his friend carried on about how nice it must be to have such a good tan." She tightened the lid on her nail polish and held out her feet, swinging them in the air. "It was like he was trying to come on to me in a backhanded sort of way."

"So . . . what did you do?"

"I went over and stood beside Stan, expecting him to be his normal, cool self . . . you know, clue this guy in on the two of us."

"Yeah?"

"But Stan clammed up. Didn't say a word in my defense. And even worse, his friend didn't seem to know when to quit."

"What else did he say?"

"Stuff like where was I during Cinco de Mayo this year and was English my second language." She sighed. "It was the cocky, sarcastic way he said it that bugged me the most. Like he thought he was better than me just because he's white."

This was so bad! I couldn't believe Stan would tolerate

something like this, especially since Andie—his girlfriend—was the victim.

"I don't blame you for being hurt," I said. "Stan knows better."

"Well, I'm not crying the blues anymore," she said, getting up. "I'm plain mad. And if I don't split this town soon, I'm gonna burst."

I could see that a change of scenery might do her good. "I'll go home and call my dad," I said, heading for my bike.

Andie hugged me before I left. "Holly, you're the best."

"I'll call you the minute I know something." I hopped onto my bike. "Don't go anywhere, okay?"

"I'll wait by the phone," she said, waving. And I knew she would.

♥　　♥　　♥

Mom was talking on the phone in the kitchen when I arrived home. She sounded pretty involved, so I didn't bother her. When twenty more minutes had passed, I went back downstairs and waved my hands in front of her face.

"Excuse me," she said to the caller, then covered the receiver with her hand. "Holly, what is it?"

"I need to use the phone. It's important."

Mom's eyes got squinty. "Well, Andie will just have to wait," she insisted.

"It's not Andie. I have to call Daddy."

"Tonight?"

"Just some last-minute stuff about the trip."

"Okay, well, I'll be done in a few minutes." She uncovered the receiver, and I could tell by the sound of things it'd be more than a few minutes before the phone was actually free.

Heading upstairs to my room, I located my journal and began to write. *Thursday, July 7: Today's been a real eye-opener. In lots of ways. I've discovered that Stan isn't half the man I thought he was, given the circumstances. He's got some weird friend named Ryan Davis, and the guy's a total loser. I can't believe what Ryan said to Andie. I mean, this is prejudice at its worst!*

I just hope Andie can work through things. I don't know what this rotten world's coming to!

I continued to write, pouring out my woes. Then I glanced at my watch. If I didn't get Mom off the phone, it would be too late to call Andie. Her dad had made a rule for the summer—she wasn't allowed to use the phone after ten o'clock at night.

I signed off in my journal and stashed it safely away in the bottom dresser drawer. Then I hurried down the hall to the stairs. Time to claim the portable phone.

Mom was yawning as I tiptoed into the kitchen, motioning to her for all I was worth. I made some hand signals to her. She nodded, smiling, catching my unspoken message.

Sitting down at the bar, I munched on a couple of snickerdoodle cookies. Mom had made a batch this morning in the cool of the day while we kids slept in. I glanced around for Carrie and Stephie. They were nowhere in sight. Thank goodness.

Mom was still engaged in animated conversation with someone—I hadn't figured out whom—so I slid off the barstool and headed downstairs to the family room. There they were, my five siblings, stretched out in various degrees of vegetation all over the carpet. Carrie and Stephie sat crosslegged in front of the coffee table, eyes glued to the TV. Mark and Phil, my younger stepbrothers—I called them brousins since they were really cousins-turned-brothers—were gobbling popcorn. Stan took up the entire sofa part of the sectional, reclining with his legs sprawled out across the length of the furniture.

"What's on TV?" I asked.

"Shh!" they answered in chorus.

Inching into the room, I saw the reason for their interest. It looked like some sci-fi show, complete with weird music. Why Stephie and Carrie were fascinated I had no idea.

"What a waste," I muttered, heading for the stairs.

That's when Stan called to me. "Hey, Holly."

I turned around to see him getting up. "What?" I said as he came over.

"How's Andie doing?" His face looked serious. No . . . he was actually worried.

"Who wants to know?"

"C'mon, Holly, don't do this."

"Don't do what? You're the one who got all this garbage with Andie started." I turned to leave.

Stan reached out and touched my arm. "Just tell me, is she okay?"

I pulled away. "If you're so worried, why don't you ask her yourself?"

"She won't talk to me," he said.

"Well"—I eyed him sarcastically—"I wonder why."

"Okay, I'll admit it, Ryan said some stupid things, but I—"

"You?" I wanted to scream. "You just stood by and let him go off like that?"

He frowned, concerned. "Is that what Andie told you?"

I nodded. "I heard it straight from her, and that's not all. Paula and Kayla thought Ryan was bad news, too."

He ran his fingers through his hair. "I didn't mean to hurt Andie."

"Okay, but what about *me*? What was all that at supper?" I turned around and ran up the stairs.

Stan didn't follow me, and it was a good thing because

Mom was just hanging up the phone. "Phone's all yours, Holly-Heart," she said. "You might want to use the hall phone upstairs. This one needs recharging, I think."

For a long-distance call, I didn't want to chance it, so I hurried upstairs, hoping the rest of the kids would stay put in front of their ridiculous intergalactic flick.

Quickly, I punched the numbers for Daddy's luxury oceanfront house. The phone rang only twice. Saundra, my stepmom, answered. "Meredith residence."

"Hey . . . uh, this is Holly. Is my dad there?"

"He's on his way home from work," she replied.

"Work . . . this late?"

"Well, you have to remember it's only eight-fifteen here, dear," she crooned into my left ear.

"Oh, I forgot." Time zones aside, I wondered why Daddy was working so late.

"Is there a message I may give him?" Saundra asked, pouring on her not-so-subtle charm.

"I guess not." I hesitated, thinking about the time crunch involved in getting Andie's plane ticket. Hmm. Maybe I'd better go ahead and chance it and get Saundra's opinion on the matter. "Well, actually, it's about my trip out there," I continued. "I was wondering if you and Daddy would mind if I brought a friend along."

"A friend?" she said. There was a delicate pause. "Sure, since Carrie's not coming, there'll be plenty of room."

"Are you sure it'll be okay with Daddy?" I asked politely. It didn't hurt to make points with the woman who pretty much ran my father's social life.

"I think your dad will be delighted to entertain you and your friend."

"Her name's Andie—short for Andrea," I said. "She's going to try and work things out on this end with her parents. I'll let you know as soon as it's definite, okay?"

"That's fine," Saundra said. I could almost see her

perfectly manicured nails wrapped around one of their expensive telephones.

"Tell Tyler I can't wait to see him and that Carrie says hi," I said, referring to Saundra's son.

"He'll certainly miss seeing her this time," she added.

"Well, I guess I'd better get going. But tell Daddy I called."

"He should be home any minute. I will."

"Okay, thanks. Good-bye."

"Good-bye, dear," she said.

I hung up, hoping Daddy wasn't becoming a workaholic or something.

Quickly, I surveyed the stairs behind me. I didn't want Stan or anyone else listening in on my next conversation— with Andie. Our plans were going to be kept private, at least for now.

"Hello?" she answered on the first ring.

"Guess what? It's all right with California," I said, excitement rising in my voice.

"Really?" She sounded ecstatic. "Your dad said it's okay?"

"My stepmom will fill him in, but she's all for it." I heard the steps creak behind me. I spun around. "Just a minute, Andie." I left the phone dangling on its cord. I crept toward the stairs and peered down. Stan was there, all right. "What're you doing?" I said.

"I need to talk to you, Holly," he said sheepishly.

"Not now. I'm busy."

Stan turned away, leaving me alone with Andie, who was waiting impatiently. "What's going on there?" she asked. "I thought I heard Stan's voice. Does he know anything about this?"

"He knows squat," I said, laughing.

"I'll talk to my parents and call you back tonight . . . before ten," she said. "Thanks, Holly, you're terrific!"

We hung up, and I danced a jig through the hallway and

into my bedroom. What a fabulous trip we were going to have!

Mom and Uncle Jack came upstairs just as I finished another set of twirls and spins. "Everything okay?" Mom asked, peeking into my room.

"Everything's perfect." I grinned at Uncle Jack, who had a long piece of celery hanging out of his mouth—complete with leafy green ends.

"We're tired," Mom said, eyeing my stepdad. "Jack's been working long hours."

"Sweet dreams," I said. "I'll make sure the crew doesn't stay up all night."

"And don't you, either," Mom said with a grin. "You might want to think about packing pretty soon."

"I'll start tomorrow."

"Good night, kiddo," Uncle Jack called, still munching on his celery stick.

"Love you," Mom said and closed their door.

Inside my room, I undressed and found my favorite pair of pj's in my drawer. It was a rosy pink tank top with pink-and-white heart shorts to match. I curled up in my canopy bed with a brand-new Marty Leigh mystery, wondering how long before Andie would call.

Nearly a half hour passed. I couldn't believe it was almost ten when I looked at my watch. That's how it was with this incredible author. She could keep you spellbound, make you forget real life even existed.

I put the book down and went into the hallway, listening for sounds from the troops below. Surely the sci-fi movie was over.

I reached for the hall phone and was surprised to hear Stan's voice on the other line. No wonder I hadn't received Andie's call. *He* was hogging the phone.

"Excuse me, Stan," I interrupted. "I'm waiting for an important call."

"Uh, is that Holly?" another voice came on the line. It sounded familiar.

"Who's this?"

"Ryan Davis," he said. "Remember, we had supper together?"

Was this guy pushing it or what!

"Hey, I really wanted to see that magazine of yours," he went on, sounding way too eager for my liking. "You know, the one with your story in it?"

I wanted to say "forget it," but bit my tongue. "Look, I'm leaving for California in a couple days," I told him. "I'm real busy. Sorry."

"Maybe we could talk about it over a Coke before you go."

I nearly choked. Who did he think he was—insulting my best friend, putting her down in front of me at supper, and now asking me out? This was outrageous!

"I'm not allowed to date," I answered. Hopefully that would change his attitude about me.

"Oh, it wouldn't be a date," he went on. "Stan could come, too, if that would make you feel better."

Nothing would make me feel better about you, I thought. *Not now, not ever!*

"I'm waiting for a call," I said, dying to hear from Andie.

"Hey, cool," Ryan said. "Anything the pretty blonde says."

I tried not to gag. Andie was right. This guy was a total nightmare!

I hung up, waiting a few seconds for Stan to do the same. Unfortunately, I could still hear him downstairs yakking with Ryan, and it really bugged me.

Finally I could stand it no longer. I grabbed my bathrobe off the back of my door and dashed downstairs.

"Get off the phone," I told Stan.

"Deal with it," he shot back, waving me out of the room.

Wanting to cut the phone cord, I stood just outside the kitchen, waiting in the dining room where Stan couldn't see me. As I expected, he took his sweet time and eventually hung up a meager three minutes before ten o'clock. He sauntered out of the kitchen, heading toward his bedroom without even speaking to me. Just as well.

Within seconds, the phone rang, and I flew to get it. "Hello?"

"Very bad news," Andie moaned. "I'm stuck in Dressel Hills forever."

"You mean you can't go?"

"Mom says no."

"What about your dad?"

"He's not home yet," she said tearfully. "Besides, he won't agree to something Mom's already vetoed." Sounded familiar.

"Well, maybe another time?"

"Probably not," she said, exhaling into the phone. "I was really living for this."

"I know," I said, trying to soothe her disappointment. "Maybe they'll change their minds."

"Dream on."

"See you tomorrow?" I said.

"Yeah, see ya."

I hung up, feeling lousy. Andie was stuck here in town. And in three days she'd be without me to protect her from that rotten Ryan Davis. Not to mention my own stepbrother.

5

The next morning I woke up earlier than usual. I heard Mom and Uncle Jack talking quietly in their bedroom, down the hall from my room.

Yesterday's events came flooding back. The ethnic slurs Ryan had made to Andie . . . the way Stan hadn't spoken up to defend her . . . and the latest blow: Andie's mom had put her foot down about California.

I crept out of bed, found my journal, then crawled back into bed. Time to tell all. *Friday, July 8: Here I am, wanting something so badly, and BAM, the wish bubble pops right in my face! Translation: I was hoping Andie could go with me to visit my dad, but things got changed around way too fast. Her mom said no. It's no good to tell Andie to talk to her dad about it. That would just make things worse in the long run.*

I laid down my pen, thinking. What if *I* were to talk to Andie's mom? Just sorta wander over there today and test the waters . . . find out why she'd decided against letting Andie go. Maybe it would open the door for some discussion. Maybe I could put her mother's fears (she probably had some; most parents did about things like this) to rest.

With a renewed sense of urgency, I bounded out of bed and headed for the bathroom. When I was dried off from my shower and wrapped in a towel, I hurried to my room again, anxious to get over to Andie's.

When I made my kitchen appearance, Mom was already scrambling eggs and frying bacon. "How'd you sleep?" Mom asked. It was her standard line. Every day.

"Morning, Sweet Toast," Uncle Jack said, shuffling through the newspaper. He had such weird nicknames for all six of us kids. And I mean *all* of us. Uncle Jack was cool that way. (The uncle part came from the fact that he'd been married to Daddy's sister before she died.) So even though he wasn't really related to Carrie and me, it felt good knowing that he loved us enough to dream up individual nicknames.

"What do you have planned for today?" Uncle Jack asked, studying me as I settled down onto the bar stool next to him.

"Not much."

"Well, I hope whatever it is, you won't forget your mother here. I think she could use some help around the house." He winked at me and reached for a glass of orange juice. "What do you think? Can you squeeze a chore or two into your social schedule?"

It wasn't *what* he said that made me want to do exactly what Uncle Jack asked, it was *how* he said it. "Sure, I'll help," I said as Mom placed a large plate of eggs and toast in front of me. "What's up?"

"Only about twenty-five loads of laundry, give or take," Mom joked. "You probably want to freshen up your summer things for your trip, too, right?"

I nodded, scooping up a forkful of eggs. "Can I run over to Andie's first?" I asked before taking a bite.

Uncle Jack turned to me. "I've got an idea. Why don't you put in a load of wash right after breakfast, and I'll drive you to Andie's on my way to work." He glanced at Mom. "Okay with you, Susan?"

"Sounds good." Mom sat down with her usual peppermint tea. "Just don't be gone too long."

"I'll catch the bus home," I said. It was perfect. Dressel Hills had public transportation via city buses—free to the public. That made getting around our little town a cinch.

Mom stirred honey from the plastic bear into her tea, humming softly. She seemed a little distant, though, like she was contemplating something important. Uncle Jack reached across and covered her hand with his big one. "What's on your mind, Cupcake?"

She smiled a whimsical smile at me. "Guess I'm just going to miss my number one girl, that's all."

"Aw, Mom, I'll be fine. You know that," I said.

"Of course you will." She brightened. "It's just such a different world out there on the West Coast." She was thinking about big cities. Mom hated them. Too many people packed into one area gave her stress. Lots of it.

Uncle Jack squeezed Mom's hand. "Holly's going to be okay," he said. "True, she's not a big city girl, but she knows how to handle herself." He nodded at me. "Right, kiddo?"

"Uncle Jack's right," I said, smiling. He sure knew how to lighten up a conversation.

He got up and carried his plate over to the sink. "Holly won't fall for some big, bad beach bum," he said more for my benefit than Mom's. "I guarantee it. Right, Angel Face?" His eyes twinkled, but I caught the serious glint behind them.

He must have heard from Mom that I'd pretty much written off the boys around here. After the way things turned out at camp, I figured it was a good idea to cool it with the boy-girl thing. Far as I was concerned, being just friends with the opposite sex was perfect at my age—almost fourteen and a half.

"That's one of the reasons why I thought it would be fun to take Andie along to California," I said glumly.

Mom's eyebrows shot up. "Andie?"

Oops! The California thing was supposed to have been

kept a secret. Except now that things were at a standstill with Andie's parents, maybe it wasn't such a big deal anymore.

I tried to laugh it off. "Well, it was a fabulous idea while it lasted," I said. "Andie asked if she could go along, so I talked to Saundra about it. She said it was fine with her, but now Andie's mom says no."

Uncle Jack came over and leaned his hands against the bar. "That's really too bad, isn't it, hon? I think Andie's going is a really terrific idea."

Two minutes later, Mom was agreeing with Uncle Jack. Yes! With both of them on our side, maybe, just maybe, Andie and I could talk her mom into letting her go. What a fabulous turn of events!

♥   ♥   ♥

It started to rain while I was at Andie's. A dismal outlook for the day. Trying to be cheerful, I helped Mrs. Martinez by dressing Chris and Jon. The twins seemed happy to see me. Andie too. But there was an underlying sense of disappointment in the air.

"It's going to be so boring around here without you, Holly," Andie blurted out when her mom left the room.

I wanted to find the bright side of things. "Maybe it'll still work out for you to come."

"Huh?" She looked at me like I was crazy. "You don't know my parents. Once they decide something, that's it."

"Well, listen to this." And I began to fill her in on Uncle Jack's reaction.

Andie beamed with anticipation. "So your stepdad liked the idea?"

"Would I kid you, girl?" I laughed. "Let me hang around your mom for a while, you know, help her out a little. Maybe the subject will come up gracefully."

Andie sighed. "Yeah, don't you wish."

I did my thing with Andie's mom, following the twins around, picking up after them, and in general, assisting with anything that would bring me in close proximity to Mrs. Martinez.

Several times the conversation touched on my California trip, but mostly in reference to my dad and the fact that he'd become a Christian recently.

"Are you looking forward to going to California?" Mrs. Martinez asked politely.

I nodded. "It's always perfect on the beach, you know, beautiful. I always feel close to God out there."

"What's your stepmother like?" she asked, rather pointedly.

I wanted to be careful about the way I described Saundra. After all, she wasn't exactly the best role model around. If I told the truth and launched into a description of my stepmom's materialism, it might limit Andie's chances of going for sure.

"Saundra and I are getting to know each other better every time we're together." What a pathetic statement. I wasn't really saying much of anything.

Andie's mom sat down at the kitchen table with Jon on her knee. "Is she starting to go to church with your dad?"

"I don't know exactly." It remained to be seen how Saundra was responding to Daddy's conversion. "The best I can do is pray for her."

"Good for you, Holly" was all Mrs. Martinez said, and since I didn't feel the timing was right, I dismissed the idea of pushing for Andie to go.

When the phone rang, I suspected it was my own mother, reminding me of my duties at home. My assumptions were correct, and reluctantly I said good-bye to Andie and to her mom before scampering out into the drizzle to catch the bus.

♥   ♥   ♥

On the ride home, I thought of the logistics involved in getting Andie's ticket in time for the Monday flight. Even if her parents agreed, it was unlikely that there would be seats available at this late date. And at such a hectic vacation time of year. Yet, something in me held out hope.

When I arrived home, Carrie and Stephie greeted me at the back door. "You're late," Carrie bossed.

"Yeah," Stephie echoed her. "We've been sorting your dirty clothes."

I pushed past them and ran down the steps to the laundry room. The place was crammed with piles of whites, colors, and darks. "You weren't kidding," I said to Mom about the dirty clothes. "This is a mess."

Mom ignored my comment. "What took so long?" she asked, her hands on her hips now. "I thought you were coming right back."

I couldn't tell her that my plan to approach Mrs. Martinez had bombed. That I'd tried to worm my way into the conversation over there, only to end up discussing Daddy's new wife. So I muttered, "Sorry, things took longer than I thought."

"Well, I hope we have *all* your dirty laundry." She glanced around. "Carrie and Stephie brought everything down from your hamper."

I wondered if my sisters had taken advantage of the moment and snooped elsewhere in my room. I could see Mom was feeling frantic about getting me ready for the trip. After all, I was going to be gone two full weeks this time.

"Have you made a list of things to take?" she asked.

"That's a switch," I said, laughing. "I'm usually the one asking you."

She nodded. "Well, I think a list would be a good idea."

"Sure, I'll make one." I started sorting through the underwear. Then I loaded the washer, sprinkling detergent around before I closed the lid.

I gathered up the next load, but Mom kept hanging around. It seemed she had something on her mind. I knew I was right when she said, "Any chance that Andie's folks might change their minds?"

I shook my head. "Probably not."

She leaned against the dryer, pushing a strand of blond hair away from her face. "I don't know why we didn't think of this earlier. Andie would be marvelous company for you." What Mom was trying to say wasn't coming out too clearly. She really meant to say that if Andie went to California with me, maybe she wouldn't be as worried about me.

Just then a fabulous plan hit me. "Do you think Andie's mom would be more open to the idea if you gave her a call?"

"Oh, I don't know about that," Mom said, backing out of the laundry room.

"Aw, come on," I said, laughing. Maybe by keeping an upbeat, cheerful attitude about this, I could get her to see the light. "Let's discuss this." Playfully, I reached for her arm.

"It's not my place to interfere with Andie's family." She let me pull her back into the room.

"But you're such good friends with her mom, and—"

"I don't think it's fair to use our friendship like that," she said. "Rosita can be a very stubborn woman at times, and I think this may be one of those times."

"But, Mom, can't you at least call her and find out why she said no? Ple-e-ase? I'll do anything, any chore you ask."

Mom folded her hands in front of her and stepped toward me, grinning. "Does this mean *that* much to you?"

I hugged her nearly off balance. "Thanks, Mom. You're so fabulous."

She cocked her head. "Oh, so now I'm your favorite word."

I tried to maintain my composure as she headed upstairs to get the portable phone. Minutes later, she came down with the phone in her hand. "I want you to hear what I say, Holly."

Strange. Mom *never* wanted us to listen in on her phone conversations. What could possibly be on her mind?

6

"Hello, Rosita? Yes, this is Susan."

I held my breath.

"How are your little ones?"

Another medium-sized pause. I could just imagine Andie's mom telling something humorous about one of the twins. Except Mom wasn't laughing.

"Oh, that's good," Mom said, nodding. "Yes, we're just fine. Thanks." A short pause. "Well, yes, Holly mentioned something about it."

About what? What did I say? I wanted to know where this conversation was headed.

"Jack and I thought it was a very good idea," Mom said, much to my surprise. Could she be referring to Andie going with me to California?

I studied Mom's face. Her eyes grew serious; her eyebrows knit into a hard frown. "I know. Sometimes things don't make a bit of sense, but if you feel that way, I understand completely." Mom glanced at me. "Well, it was no picnic the first time I let Holly go out there, but I guess letting go is a rather slow process."

There was an exceedingly long silence on this end. Mom shook her head from time to time, but nothing more.

"What?" I whispered, but Mom waved at me to be still. This was *so* agonizing, standing here in the middle of the laundry room, listening to Mom discuss my summer plans with my best friend's mother.

The rinse cycle came on with a whooshing sound as water sprayed against spinning clothes. The noise triggered the end of Mom's conversation with Mrs. Martinez. She said she'd talk with her again. I couldn't wait for Mom to hang up. Maybe then I'd get some straight answers at last.

Finally she beeped the phone off. "What?" I demanded. "What did Andie's mom say?"

"Holly-Heart," Mom said, smiling, "I think you can relax about the whole thing."

"What are you saying?"

She sighed. "Rosita's just a little fearful, that's all." She placed the phone on top of the dryer. "There's really no logical reason for her to have said no, but who knows, maybe next year. Things like this take time."

"Time?" I was beside myself. Here we were, approaching the goal, and Mom was talking about our biggest enemy. "We don't *have* time!"

She smiled. "We do if you want this thing to work itself out."

Mom was probably right. Again. "So . . . how long do we have to wait?"

Her eyes twinkled. "Only until Rosita calls a travel agent. How's that?"

"Oh, Mom!" I ran to her open arms.

"Happy?" she whispered.

I showed her just how very happy with the biggest bear hug I could muster.

Hours later, Andie's mom called back. She'd gotten the information she needed. It was celebration time. Which, unfortunately, only lasted five seconds.

Turned out the Monday flight was booked—not a single

coach ticket available. Which meant Andie would have to fly standby or not go at all—her mom said she really didn't want Andie traveling alone for her first flight. Don't ask me why; after all, I've seen lots of much younger kids flying alone. But Mom had said Rosita was stubborn, and boy was she right.

♥ ♥ ♥

Saturday, Mom and I met Andie and her mom at the Soda Straw for lunch. Mom said it was just going to be a little get-together before Andie and I left town. No big deal. Well, what was supposed to be no big deal turned out to be a mini-lecture, more for Andie's benefit than for mine. And at one point during the conversation—even before the waitress had a chance to bring us our burgers and fries—Mrs. Martinez asked me point-blank if I would watch over Andie.

Who did she think I was? Andie's worst enemy? Of course I'd be looking out for my friend, and I said so.

Andie's mom eyed me quite seriously. "Now you know that Andrea has never been away from home like this before. She's very naïve."

And I'd like her to stay that way, Mrs. Martinez was probably thinking.

I nodded, trying to avoid looking at Andie. We both knew her mother's image of California had come from the media. White sand, tanned bodies, wild beach parties . . . the whole sun and surf thing. I didn't want my laughter spilling out while she was speaking so directly and seriously to me. I respected Mrs. Martinez and her feelings; still, there was just a little too much hovering going on at the moment.

"Andrea has led a sheltered life," she continued. "You know what I'm saying?"

Of course I knew. Andie and I were in the same boat when it came to being a bit overly protected. Personally, I didn't mind. It beat having more freedom than you can handle, like most teens I knew.

Andie's mom gave her daughter a molasses-sweet look. "Andrea's mostly naïve about boys, you know." She switched her gaze to me. "Except for your stepbrother Stan she's never really dated. And since she's only fourteen—"

"Almost fifteen," Andie interrupted.

"Well, almost, yes, but nevertheless, you're much too young for boy-girl nonsense." Mrs. Martinez leaned back against the red vinyl booth. Her eyebrows had been waxed to a narrow line, framing her large deep-set eyes nicely. When she frowned, as she was now, the too-thin eyebrows made her eyes look almost mournful.

I could tell she was desperate. She wanted a firm commitment from me—something she could count on to make her feel more comfortable.

"I'll take good care of Andie," I volunteered, meaning it.

"I can take care of myself," Andie spouted.

Mrs. Martinez rolled her eyes exactly the way Andie always did. "Now, Andrea," she whispered.

Mom leaned forward at that moment. "Holly's made some nice friends at her father's house. I don't think we have to worry. The main thing is for the two of you to stick together. Don't go pairing off with boys"—and here she looked directly at me. "Holly doesn't car-date yet, either, so you girls are on your honor."

"We'll be just fine," I assured both mothers. And I had no doubt that we would.

When the door jingled, I looked up. Jared Wilkins and Billy Hill strolled inside. They waved when they spotted us in the corner booth—the same one Jared and I had shared over a year ago when we'd first met.

Jared was the last person I wanted to see today. He and I

were still friends, sort of, but I didn't want to be tied down to one boy anymore. The boy-girl thing had gotten too complicated last school year, and I just wanted to cool it. Not only with Jared—with all guys.

"Hey," he said, coming over. Billy waved, looking a little shy when he realized we were with our moms. Jared wasn't bashful, though. "Looks like you've got a cozy mother-daughter event going here. Nice to see you again, Mrs. Meredith . . . er, Patterson."

"Same to you, Jared," Mom said politely, ignoring the mistake with her new married name.

"How are your little boys?" he asked Andie's mom. "Chris and Jon, right?"

Mrs. Martinez nodded. "Lively as ever."

I smiled. Andie didn't. She was still ticked, I think, at what had happened at youth camp last month. It was a very long story, but as far as I was concerned, all was forgiven.

"So, what's the occasion?" Jared asked.

"It's our farewell lunch," I said. "Andie's going with me to California on Monday."

Billy piped up. "Really?"

"That's the plan," Andie said, grinning.

Jared flashed his dimples at me. "Well, have fun."

"We sure will." I wanted to reinforce my stand, in case he thought I'd softened on my decision.

"See ya," Jared said, and he and Billy headed to the counter to order.

♥   ♥   ♥

Later that evening, Andie and I sat on my front-porch swing talking between slurps of root beer floats.

Ryan had come by to pick up Stan about thirty minutes

before. They were going to see some show downtown.

Andie looked like she was going to pop. But I knew there was no way she'd hold her breath for an apology from either Ryan or Stan. If Stan had any smarts, he'd certainly have offered a humble one. And Ryan? He was as rude as they come.

After the guys left, Andie spewed out her feelings.

"I guess my mom was right. I *have* been sheltered." She sat cross-legged on the porch swing next to me. "At least I've never had to deal with any sort of prejudice before. Never." She continued to rant about Ryan's slurs, rehashing the scene at the Y a few days ago. "Just where do you think Stan was during all that?" She huffed. "It was like he was totally out to lunch instead of standing right there beside me."

"I know," I said, touching her shoulder. "I know."

"Just when you think you've found a guy you can really be friends with, something like this has to happen."

"Mom says there's lots of good fish in the sea," I said, trying to comfort her.

"Yeah, right. The problem is *finding* the fish."

"Don't worry about that. We'll pray 'em in."

She turned to look at me. "You honestly pray about everything, don't you?"

"Close." It was true. For some reason I talked to God about most everything.

Andie played with the chain on the porch swing, deep in thought. "Sometimes God answers with 'no,' sometimes a 'maybe' . . . not always a 'yes.' At least, that's what Pastor Rob says."

I nodded. "Bottom line, though, He knows what's best for us. I guess, for some people, trusting is the hardest part."

Silently, we contemplated the fact. Andie seemed restless about something, though, and when I mentioned it, she asked, "What are my chances of actually making that flight, really?"

I should've known. . . .

"Don't worry," I said casually. "I've seen zillions of passengers get on with standby status."

"Honest?" Her eyes lit up.

I nodded. But deep down, where my greatest fears always simmered before surfacing, I knew this standby thing was very tricky.

Andie *had* to get on my flight. Or else we were right back where we started.

7

Denver International Airport was wildly congested.
Vacation season was in full swing, and crowds of people
flocked to the enormous airport east of the big city. Andie
and I waited near one of the many automatic doors, juggling
luggage, while Uncle Jack drove the van to the short-term
parking area. At the last minute, he'd decided to drive us
instead of Mom because he had some business to tend to at
his Denver office. The car trip from Dressel Hills to Denver
zoomed by surprisingly fast, and all because of Uncle Jack's
continuous flow of airplane jokes.

"Bet you're going to miss your stepdad, huh?" Andie said
as we waited.

"There's no one quite like Uncle Jack, that's for sure."

She squeezed her gym bag. "I can't wait to see your dad
again . . . your real dad. It'll be so great to see what *he's* like
now."

I spied Uncle Jack outside, hurrying across the street.
"Oh, you'll like Daddy. He's very articulate—handsome,
too—but he doesn't joke around a lot." *He doesn't have time
to; he works too much,* I thought.

My uncle helped us lug our bags into the long line where
I'd be checking mine. The plan was that Andie would carry

her single bag onto the plane—that is, if she even got on.

At last we were past security, where Uncle Jack was given a pass, allowing him to escort us to the gate. Then we headed for the underground tram and on toward the correct concourse, keeping our eyes peeled for gate eleven. Uncle Jack helped navigate while Andie chattered like a chipmunk. This was her first flight anywhere. She was acting like a kid about to eat her first ice-cream cone.

"Oh, Holly, this is going to be so amazing." She grabbed my arm as we walked.

I agreed. "Maybe you'll get hooked on flying and want to fly all over the place."

When we located gate eleven, the waiting area was crammed with people. Andie and I searched for three seats together, with no luck. Uncle Jack saved the day and discovered two vacant seats close to the window. "Here you go," he said. "Window seats for the ladies." He waited till we got situated before excusing himself to make a phone call.

Andie and I whispered and giggled nonstop—a preview of what was surely ahead for us in California. "Just think, we've got two whole weeks away from our mundane, boring Dressel Hills lives," she said. "When we're old and crotchety, we'll be telling our grandkids about this trip."

"Oh, did I tell you? My dad has passes to Universal Studios," I said, suddenly remembering.

Andie's eyebrows leaped up. "Really? When did this happen?" Before I could answer, she said, "What else haven't you told me?"

"Absolutely nothing." I scratched my head and put on a frown. "Oh, yeah, I forgot to tell you about my wicked stepmother. I figured you wouldn't want to come along if I said anything. But now that you're committed to going—"

"Holly, you never call her that," she interrupted, glancing around to see if anyone was listening.

I lowered my voice and leaned closer to Andie. "You'll be

calling her wicked, too, when you find out what she makes you do."

She giggled. "Don't be silly."

"Okay." I folded my arms across my chest. "But don't say I didn't warn you."

She cocked her head at me, trying to decide if what I'd said was to be taken sincerely.

I shook my head, keeping a straight face. "Yep, Saundra will have you cleaning out cupboards and closets all week long. Oh, and she likes the pantry alphabetized according to brand names."

"You're kidding," she said, a tiny smirk waiting in the wings.

"You just better hope you make this flight so you can see for yourself."

"I don't believe you." She was about to toss her gym bag at me when the announcement came for first-class passengers to board the airplane. I felt my stomach lurch. This was it. We'd know in a few minutes whether Andie was coming or not.

I grabbed her hand. "Have you prayed about this?"

"Me? I thought you were the one doing all the praying."

"But this was *your* idea, right?" I stared at her. "Well, don't you think you ought to?"

"Okay, I'll pray," she said, bowing her head right there in front of everyone. Her lips started moving, and I could see that she was squeezing her folded hands like crazy. Andie wanted this trip bad. I remembered lots of times when I couldn't get her to pray over her food in public, but this . . .

She was really going at it. I sent a powerful silent prayer heavenward as I got up and headed over to the check-in counter. "Excuse me," I said to the man dressed in a navy blue uniform. "Could you please tell me if there are any no-shows for the coach section?" I explained that Andie was flying standby and wondered what her chances were.

"Just one moment, miss." He pulled up the information on the computer. His eyes darted back and forth, scanning the screen. "Looks like there are three no-shows so far." He smiled a comforting smile. "But your friend will have to wait until all passengers have boarded before we can give her the go-ahead."

"Thank you very much." I was more hopeful than ever and hurried over to Andie, who was still squeezing her eyes shut in earnest prayer. I touched her hand. "I think God heard and answered already."

"Oh, Holly, this is so cool." She hugged the living daylights out of me.

I pulled back, filling her in on the details. "Let's wait to celebrate until you're on the plane, okay?"

She turned around and stared out the window overlooking the runways. The plane—our plane—was a DC-10. We watched as the luggage carriers glided along the ground loading the luggage.

"Hey, look." I pointed. "There's my suitcase."

Andie leaned forward. "You're right."

The large piece of pink yarn tied to the suitcase handle would make it easy to spot in L.A. I'd gotten the idea from one of Marty Leigh's mystery books. One of her characters obsessed over identifying her own luggage. She decorated it with brightly colored ribbons and yarn. Every piece, every time.

That's when I heard the announcement for standby passengers. I felt tense, jittery—tried to picture Andie walking down the long, narrow Jetway to board the plane with me.

I glanced around, checking on the short line of standby passengers filing down the enclosed walkway connecting the terminal to the plane. "Shouldn't be long now," I whispered, half to myself, half to Andie.

The names of a Rudy and Jayne Kish were called over the intercom. I watched the young couple hurry to the podium and show their IDs. Promptly, they were given a boarding pass and returned to their seats.

Andie's eyes filled with worry. "How much longer . . . before my name is called?"

"And it *will* be, you know," I assured her.

Uncle Jack strolled to the window, his hands in his pants pockets. I wondered if he was as concerned as I was. Actually, I'd never seen my uncle freak out over anything. He was calm and cool, the way I wished I could be. Especially now.

Soon, another standby passenger was called to the podium.

My pulse raced. I could scarcely breathe. And just when I thought I'd burst, another name was announced. A tall, good-looking man hurried to the check-in counter.

Andie grabbed my arm and clung to it. "Oh, Holly," she moaned. "I can't stand the suspense."

"We're *both* getting on this flight. I can feel it." I let Andie hang on to me as the beady-eyed man in uniform offered a boarding pass to the tall man.

About that time, Uncle Jack wandered over to us, checking his watch. "The flight's scheduled for departure at 12:15. That's twenty-five minutes from now."

"So . . . I'll know soon if I'm going or not," Andie said softly.

First-class passengers were invited to board. Then coach passengers, beginning with rows twenty-five to thirty-three. A bunch of people lined up in response to the announcement. Parents with small children, older folk, men in business suits.

Still, I wanted to hold out for a miracle.

"I can't believe this," Andie was saying, tears in her eyes. "I guess this is good-bye."

We were both in tears, and Uncle Jack came over and put his arm around Andie as he leaned over to kiss my cheek. "Don't let this ruin your time, sweetie," he said. Then, turning to Andie, he winked at her. "Hey, kiddo, you and me—let's paint the town, okay?"

Uncle Jack was so cool. He would see to it that Andie had a fabulous day. She'd probably end up having more fun than I'd have the whole two weeks.

"Better get in line now, Holly," Uncle Jack said. "They won't hold your plane forever."

"Bye. Love you." I hugged my stepdad and then Andie again. "You too!"

"Send me lots of emails, okay?" Andie said.

"I'll write at least twice a day."

After showing my boarding pass and ID, I hurried down the walkway. I wiped my cheeks, too upset to look back.

Andie wasn't coming with me to California. God had said no this time. But why?

Down the long ramp, I headed toward the plane. Maybe God had something else planned for Andie. I could only hope it was something wonderful.

Just as I was about to enter the plane, the tall, handsome man—the last standby passenger called—was being escorted out of the plane by a male flight attendant. Evidently there was a problem. The name on his boarding pass didn't match the name on his checked lugguge, so he had to get off the plane. His luggage would have to be removed, as well!

"Excuse me," I said to the flight attendant. "Does this mean there's room for one more standby passenger on this flight?"

The uniformed attendant nodded. "Only one." He headed up the ramp with the ousted passenger.

Wow. This was so fabulous. I didn't know what to do first. But I knew I had to run back up the Jetway and let Andie know this good news.

"Miss," the flight attendant said as I passed him, "if you haven't boarded by the time the door is closed on the plane, you will miss your flight."

So I hurried to the waiting area and looked around. Andie and Uncle Jack were nowhere in sight!

Rushing to the podium, I was out of breath. "Can you please page someone for me?" Quickly, I filled him in about Andie needing to go to California with me, how she'd already left with my stepdad to head for the terminal. "She thinks the plane is filled, but it's not."

"One moment, please." He checked the monitor, then nodded with a smile.

I heard Andie's name over the entire airport intercom. Darting out into the wide concourse, I searched frantically. People crowded my vision, making it impossible to spot Andie. Or Uncle Jack.

My heart pounded uncontrollably. This was worse than any nightmare I'd *ever* had!

8

The attendant frowned. "Now, young lady, if you don't go this instant, you, too, will miss your plane."

I had no choice. Daddy and Saundra would be waiting for me at the L.A. airport. If I didn't show up they'd be very worried. So, with great reluctance, I obeyed.

The flight attendant brightened when he saw me coming. "Oh, good, you're back."

"Uh, they're paging my friend right now. Is there any way you can hold the plane for her?"

"Is your friend the Queen of England?"

I caught the joke, but it wasn't funny. I tried to explain my problem, but he couldn't give me any reason to hope that Andie would catch this plane.

He asked to see my ticket. "You're in row seventeen, seat C."

My heart sank as I made my way through first class—all those comfortable, spacious seats were filled. In fact, the entire plane was filled to capacity. Except for one aisle seat five rows into the coach section. I nearly cried as I passed it. It could've been Andie's seat. If only . . .

I couldn't stop thinking about her. Even if she and Uncle Jack *had* heard the page, it was unlikely that she could make it in time. Not the way the concourses were crowded. Not the way the flight attendant glowered when I asked if they could please hold the plane.

I found my seat. It was also on the aisle, and every few seconds I leaned around the seat in front of me, hoping to spot Andie.

A flight attendant came down the aisle, offering magazines. Who could read at a time like this? Instead, I prayed under my breath, begging God to please change His mind about things.

I remembered how Andie had bowed her head in prayer inside the concourse. It was one of the few times she'd ever done such a thing—closing her eyes like that in public—and I asked God to reward Andie for her courage. For her faith. To give her this trip she longed for.

I said "amen" audibly, not caring what the lady beside me thought. When I opened my eyes, I couldn't believe it. There was Andie Martinez in the flesh. Trooping down the aisle as though she owned the place.

"Yes," I said, leaping up. "Andie!"

Her face burst into an enormous grin. She waved triumphantly and sat down just as the second officer's voice came over the intercom. "Flight attendants, prepare for cross-check."

I fastened my seat belt, making sure it was tight. What an incredible day.

♥ ♥ ♥

When the plane leveled off at peak altitude, the seat belt sign was turned off and passengers were allowed to move around. Andie didn't waste any time getting out of her seat.

She stood in the aisle beside my seat, beaming. "Is this incredible or what?"

"I know. I mean, here I was coming to get on the plane, and I find out that tall guy isn't getting on, after all. So, I make a mad dash back up to find you, and you're gone!"

Her eyes danced with excitement. "You must've been totally freaked."

"Worse," I said, remembering the panic.

"Well"—she handed me a note—"read this while I use the rest room."

"Thanks." I felt like at least a zillion bucks as I opened her note.

> Hey, Holly,
>   This is just too cool. I'm really going to California with you! Can you believe it?
>   You were right about trusting God and all. It really looked like He'd said "No"—loud and clear—but this . . . this is so-o-o totally cool. I think between the two of us, our prayers got answered. Pronto!
>   Oh, yeah. You should've seen your uncle Jack's face when we heard my name being paged. Actually, he was the one who made it possible for me to catch this plane. He grabbed a luggage cart, I hopped in, and he pushed me faster than lightning back to gate 11. It was so weird. I'm glad you have such a great stepdad. And, in case you didn't know it . . . you're not so bad yourself!
>   Love ya, kid,
>   Andie

I refolded her note, smiling. What a sight they must have been, flying down the concourse like that with Andie in a luggage cart.

When she finally came back down the aisle, I stopped her. "I have a fabulous idea. Let's write notes."

"You're on," she said, trotting back to her seat.

I pulled a fresh piece of lined paper out of my backpack.

I always carried a small six-by-nine-inch tablet with me. Essential equipment for a writer.

> *Dearest Andie,*
>
> *You won't believe this, but while you were racing to catch this plane, I was praying. I asked God to reward you for praying in public. Remember back there when you prayed while we were waiting to find out about this flight?*
>
> *I know it was probably tough for you, but I was really proud. I'm sure God was, too!*
>
> *Hey, this is weird. I almost feel like we're in Mr. Ross's science class passing notes. Now you owe me one.*
>
> *Friends forever,*
Holly

We passed notes back and forth while the flight attendants served us pretzels and a beverage. But afterward, I started feeling wiped out. Andie, however, was wired up and ready for anything. I had to talk her into letting me catch some zs during the remainder of the trip. It wasn't easy.

"How can you sleep when we're in the middle of a miracle?" she said when she passed my seat on her way back from returning a magazine.

I yawned. "Ever hear of adrenaline depletion?"

"Oh, that."

"Yeah, that," I said. "Traveling with you is exhausting."

She actually gave up and let me rest.

♥ ♥ ♥

Much later I had the privilege of introducing Andie to Daddy, Saundra, and Tyler at the L.A. airport. They seemed pleased that she had come. Daddy was especially interested in hearing about God's answer to our prayers. Saundra didn't seem to care.

Once we arrived at the luxurious beach house, Andie and I began settling in. I showed her down the vine-entangled spiral staircase—I called it the Cinderella stairs—to the guest bedrooms. We had two spacious rooms, each opening to a large, cozy sitting room where bookshelves were filled with classics and poetry. And a complete set of the Marty Leigh mystery series. Along with a desk and chair where quiet thoughts could be recorded, there was a big-screen TV and an entertainment system to boot.

After I gave Andie the tour of the lower level, we made quick work of unpacking. She was anxious to swim in the Pacific Ocean. "Do you realize, Holly Meredith, that I'm nearly fifteen years old and I've never seen the ocean?" She was already changing into her bathing suit.

I sat in a leather recliner near the windows, drinking in the spectacular view of the blue Pacific. "The water's salty," I told her. "You shouldn't swallow if you get any in your mouth."

"Yes, mother." She came over to have another look.

I glanced at her. She was spunky, all right.

"Whew, it feels good putting a couple of states between me and that lousy Ryan whatever-his-face-is."

"Yeah," I said, watching the sea gulls swoop and sway in the distance. "I wonder what Stan sees in him as a friend."

"Beats me," Andie said, investigating the room. There was an oil painting of the tall red-topped lighthouse at St. George's Reef on the wall opposite the window. "Wow," she whispered. "This picture looks expensive."

"It's an original."

She moved close to the painting. "How can you tell?"

"See the artist's brush strokes?"

"Yeah, I see what you mean." Then she stepped back, surveying the whole room. "Man, your dad must be rich."

I nodded, content to sit in the comfortable chair. "I suppose so."

She looked at me with surprise in her eyes. "You mean you don't know for sure?"

"It doesn't matter, really. Besides, I don't want to get into this right now." The whole thing with Daddy coming out here when Mom didn't want to move, back before their divorce, well, sometimes it still hurt. Like now.

Thank goodness Andie understood. She took my lead and dropped the subject. "Well, I'm ready to hit the beach. You coming?"

"Give me five." I pulled myself out of the chair and hurried through the sitting room to my own room. Inside the room, which was decorated in creams and greens, I closed the door. Andie and I would probably end up discussing my feelings about Daddy's remarriage sometime while we were here. But . . . maybe not. I just wished it hadn't come up right off the bat like this.

Locating my swimsuit, I put it on, taking my time. I could almost feel the vibrations coming from Andie's room, she was so hyper.

I sighed. Hopefully she'd slow down a bit. Maybe a good swim in the ocean was what she needed.

With towels and a beach ball in hand, we dashed to the sandy path. It sloped down a bit, leveled off, then dipped a little, leading us to the beach.

It was a fine, hot day, complete with a balmy ocean breeze. Eagerly we marked our territory with giant towels given to us by Saundra. They were thick ones; felt new. My stepmom wanted only the best for us.

We used our sandals to anchor our towels; then, with total abandon, we raced to the ocean. The waves called to me, and I swam out past the breakers. Andie followed.

"I'm never going home!" she shouted as we floated free and easy under the California sun.

"I know. This place is total heaven."

She grinned at me, riding a low swell. "Do you think there's an ocean in heaven?"

"Well," I said, thinking, "there's the sea of forgetfulness where God dumps our sins. How's that?"

"But I want waves." She giggled blissfully.

We let the tide pull us closer to the beach, where giant waves picked us up like tiny corks bobbing in the water. What a fabulous way to spend the afternoon.

Later, we decided to get some sun. Andie was already tan, her natural skin color, but I was whiter than white. Since the sun was still fairly high, I knew I'd better get some sunscreen. "I'll be right back," I said. "Need anything?"

"Some music would be nice," she said, turning over on her stomach.

"I'll see if Daddy has a radio we can borrow." I hurried up the worn path to the house and climbed the steps to the deck. I wiped the sand off my feet before I entered through the sliding glass doors.

Inside, Saundra was stirring something on the stove. I wondered if Daddy had gone back to work. Probably. I crept into the open, distinctly modern kitchen. "I'm sorry to bother you, but could I borrow some sunscreen?"

"Certainly, dear. I have some in my bathroom just above the sink. You're welcome to it." Saundra pointed me in the direction of hers and Daddy's bedroom.

The room had a dazzling Victorian decor complete with ecru lace curtains. I studied the cameo fan design on each window panel. The profile was an old-fashioned lady with her hair swept up similar to Saundra's. The walls were the same cream color, with a shaped wallpaper border running around the ceiling.

And the bed. It was king size with eyelet shams atop a lace-edged comforter that picked up the Victorian fan theme in tans, browns, and rosy hues.

On the far wall stood a wide dresser with hand-stenciled fans centered on each drawer. A white castlelike birdhouse sat to the left of the mirror. The room made me almost forget what I was looking for.

Sunscreen. Yes, that's why I was in this magical place. I moved quickly to the large bathroom, trying to ignore its uncommon beauty. Opening the medicine cabinet, I located the sun block easily. As I reached for it, my hand bumped a container of pills. The plastic bottle clattered into the sink below.

I picked it up. *Robert Meredith* was printed on it. What was *this*?

Quickly, I slipped the pills back into the cabinet and left the room. Back in the kitchen, Saundra was still stirring noodles. I stood there, wondering if I should inquire about Daddy's pills.

Tyler came up behind me in the hallway. "How's the water?" he asked, glancing toward the ocean.

"Oh, Andie's having a fabulous time," I said. "It's her first visit to the ocean, you know."

"Really? Way cool."

Saundra looked up just then. Her reddish hair was drawn back in a fancy hair clip at her neck. "Is there anything else I can get you for your swim?"

"Well, Andie just wondered if you have a portable radio, that's all."

Tyler seemed eager to help. "You can borrow mine." He disappeared down the hall to his room.

Saundra's silver hoop earrings danced as she stirred the pasta. "I hope you and Andie like spaghetti and meatballs."

"Sounds delicious, thanks." I wondered about the lack of excitement in her voice. "Everything all right?" I ventured.

She smiled, her lips bright with red lipstick, one of her trademarks. But she avoided my question. "How soon do you think you girls will be ready for supper?"

"Whenever you want to eat will be fine," I replied. But I had something else on my mind. I inched farther into the kitchen, wondering how to approach Saundra with my concern. "Where's Daddy?"

"He had to finish up some work at the office. He'll be back later, dear." She reached up and turned on the fan above the stove. It seemed to signify the end of our conversation.

Tyler returned with his box radio. "Here you go." He gave me his radio complete with CD player. Slung over his shoulder was a medium-sized pouch. "Thought you might wanna listen to some of my CDs, too."

"Whatcha got?"

"Oh, a little country . . . a little R and B."

"Thanks," I said and headed back outdoors. Saundra's son, now ten, never ceased to amaze me. He was perceptive, thoughtful, and much more grown-up than most kids his age.

I wondered if Daddy had taken Tyler to church with him yet. Tyler had shown some interest in God, openly discussing things like prayer and the creation of the world when I'd visited last. When Saundra wasn't around, of course. Daddy had said once that she didn't believe in a personal God. So I assumed Tyler didn't, either.

I tucked the sunscreen under my arm, leaving my hands free to carry the boom box. Like everything else in Daddy's house, this, too, was probably expensive.

Part way down the sandy slope leading to the beach, I noticed a guy in purple-and-blue surfer pants talking to Andie. He was tall, Hispanic, and bare-chested . . . and he was sitting on *my* beach towel.

Andie's eyes danced with excitement when she saw me. "You're back!" She seemed elated.

What was she so happy about? I glanced down at Tyler's radio. Maybe it was the possibility of music on the beach. Then I saw a familiar glint in the guy's eyes as he grinned at

Andie. Oh, so *that's* what it was. . . .

Andie waved me over. "Holly, you're just in time to meet Rico Hernandez."

"Hey," I said, wishing she wouldn't do this. Introductions to perfect strangers were always awkward for me. Besides, I wanted to get on with our afternoon. Andie's and mine.

She turned and smiled up at him like she'd known him all her life. "Rico, this is my friend Holly Meredith."

"Hey." He glanced up at me, still perched on my beach towel.

I got a better look. And cringed. This guy—this *stranger*—was at least eighteen!

9

Honestly, I didn't know what to say or think.

I tried to figure out how long I'd been gone. Ten minutes, max. By the looks of things, Andie had gone and flipped over a complete stranger in the time it took me to go for sun block.

"Time for music." I set the CD player down on the sand because there was no room on my towel. Rico only had eyes for Andie, so it still hadn't hit him that he was trespassing on my spot.

"Thanks," Andie said, as though I'd hauled the boom box out here for their exclusive use.

Rico found the tuner and scanned the airwaves. His wet hair glistened in the sun. "What's your style?" He was facing Andie.

"You pick," she said, grinning at me. I gave her my cut-throat gesture, which meant cool-it-with-this-guy-and-let's-get-on-with-our-plans, but it didn't seem to register.

I was about to leave to get another towel when Rico suddenly snapped to it and remembered his manners. Leaping up, he sputtered, "Here, have a seat."

"Thanks." But I didn't feel comfortable shooting the

breeze with a guy neither of us knew. Why wasn't Andie being more cautious?

It wasn't like Rico looked suspicious or anything. And I couldn't imagine him turning out to be a serial killer, but what was he doing hanging out with fourteen-year-olds?

Rico turned to Andie, then me. "You wanna see something cool?"

"Sure," Andie exclaimed.

"Like what?" I said.

"Up there," he pointed, "at the high tide, there's lots of shells packed in the sand. Wanna see?"

"That's okay," I said, "you go ahead." And surprise, surprise, Andie got up and off they went, leaving me to deal with what sounded like a rumba blaring over Tyler's radio.

"Don't be long," I called to Andie, lying on my stomach facing the water. "Supper's almost ready."

I sounded just like Mom. Which reminded me of my promise to Andie's mother. I'd told her I would watch out for Andie while we were here. And watch her I did. Pretending to sunbathe, I spied on my best friend—watched her walk barefooted in the foamy surf. The wind made a point of tossing her curls against her face now and then. I heard her laughter, too. Rico was much taller than she, but her height didn't seem to matter. I watched him kneel in the sand, showing Andie how to skip stones into the receding tide. It was a scene for a painting. And my friend looked happier than I'd seen her in ages.

I remembered her tears after the Ryan Davis incident. And Stan doing zilch about it made things even worse.

Pushing my pointer finger into the sand, I dug a tiny hole, feeling a little lonely . . . and wondering about Rico Hernandez.

♥   ♥   ♥

At supper, Andie was quiet, subdued. I wondered what she was thinking. But, really, I knew. Rico was already part of her thought processes. I could see it in her eyes. Recalling the way he'd looked at her all afternoon, though, made me even more nervous.

Daddy's chair remained vacant until the tail end of supper. Finally he arrived, rushing into the kitchen just as Saundra was dishing up dessert—warm apple pie with ice cream on the side.

"Hello, dear," he said with a quick kiss. He looked at Andie and me. "Well, how was your first day in sunny California, girls?"

I wished he hadn't asked. Surely Andie wouldn't launch off on her latest romantic interest. I decided not to give her the opportunity. "Well, we're completely unpacked and settled." I sent Andie an eyeful. She caught it this time and kept her mouth shut. "I took Andie out for a long swim."

"So you got a taste of our ocean," he remarked.

"You could say that," I said.

Tyler talked about his summer school class for a while before Daddy began to talk about his work. Saundra listened attentively, but she couldn't hide the concern in her eyes. What did she know about Daddy that I didn't?

Andie and I sat politely long after our dessert was finished. It was Tyler who brought up the question of going to Universal Studios.

Daddy leaned back in his chair. "Well, we can go any day you'd like. What do you think, hon?"

Saundra tapped her long manicured nails on the tabletop. They matched the red on her lips. "I think it would probably work best on Friday."

"Friday's out," he said. "I have to be at the office all day."

One glance at Saundra's face told me she was disappointed. "Weren't you going to take some time off this week?" I could almost imagine the last part of her sentence.

The part she'd left out: *while your daughter's here?*

He looked uncomfortable. "I'll have to make up for the time on Saturday." He didn't look at me. "Friday it is, then."

Tyler clapped his hands. "Yes!" he shouted.

That little problem settled, Andie and I began clearing the table. Saundra actually let us help, which was highly unusual. In fact, I was convinced by the unspoken words at the table just now that maybe Daddy and Saundra needed some time alone. So I volunteered to finish up the kitchen. "We'll put everything away for you," I said.

Saundra smiled and put her arm around Daddy. "Thanks, Holly, you're a dear."

"Yes, Holly, you're such a dear," Andie said impishly when they'd gone. Tyler snickered, but I didn't say anything.

I waited till he'd cleared the table and left the room before I spoke. "I think we have to talk," I began. "And I think you know what about."

She tossed her head from side to side comically. "If it's about alphabetizing the canned goods, forget it."

"Very cute."

"No, really, I don't think your stepmom's all that wicked."

"Shh!"

"You mean she doesn't *know* she's a wicked stepmother?" Andie was really sneaky. Trying to get me off the subject.

"Andie," I tried again. "Just listen to me."

She was leaning over the dishwasher but remained motionless like a statue.

Exasperated, I turned around, my hands all soapy. "Stand up and listen."

She cranked herself up slowly like a windup doll. "There, how's that?"

I turned around and finished wringing out the dishcloth. "You're hopeless."

"I am?"

"Yeah, just forget it." I wasn't in the mood to approach

her about Rico Hernandez. Not anymore. Mostly because I could see she was euphoric. And he was the reason.

We worked in silence, finishing off the kitchen in nothing flat. Andie was smarter than to push the issue. After all, she and I had been best friends for as long as I could remember, so she probably already figured out what I was thinking.

Both of us phoned home to our families to let them know we'd arrived safely. When Andie talked to her mom, I noticed she purposely left Rico out of the conversation. She kept asking her mom to repeat things. Probably because her twin brothers were crying in the background.

After she hung up, Andie cornered me near the refrigerator. "Holly, I want you to promise not to tell my mom about Rico."

"Sure, fine, whatever," I said glibly. "What's to tell?"

"I really like him, Holly. We're so much alike." Her eyes, normally quite round, grew narrow now. Almost slits. "I know you're my best friend, but I need to hear you say, 'I promise.' "

Not only was she glaring at me, she was squeezing my arm!

"Why? What's going on?"

"Nothing, but you know how my mom is . . . she jumps to all sorts of ridiculous conclusions. So, will you promise?"

"What's the big deal?" I said.

"It's important to me, that's what."

I could see she wasn't going to let this go till I gave in. "Okay," I reluctantly agreed. "I promise."

"Good." She looked perfectly relieved.

Tyler called to us from the living room, wanting us to play Monopoly. "C'mon, girls, I'll take you on."

"You're no match for me," Andie said.

I laughed. "Just you wait." We settled down for an evening of popcorn and Park Avenue.

Daddy came in later, wearing his robe and slippers. Saundra

seemed awfully attentive to him, plumping the cushions behind his overstuffed chair and helping him find just the right position for his footrest. Then she put on some soft music in the background, lit all the candles in the room, and dimmed the lights.

"Mom!" Tyler wailed. "We can't see our game."

She tilted her head as if to say she was sorry and turned the lights up just a bit. "There, dear, how's that?"

"Still too dark," he said, sounding less spoiled than before. "But we'll live with it."

I grinned at Andie. This kid had his mom wrapped around both his little fingers. Not only that, he wiped Andie off the board within the first hour of play.

I hung in there, with some cheering from Andie. Daddy, too.

Shaking the dice, I held my breath for a nine. A six, seven, eight, or ten meant certain bankruptcy. Shoot, any other number meant I was headed to the poorhouse. Tyler owned so many hotels he couldn't fit all of them on the board. I wondered if living with a tycoon stepfather had made any difference.

"Throw!" Tyler rubbed his hands together, anticipating his triumph. One die rolled off the board, and Tyler cupped his hands over it. "A six!"

The other die was a two. Game over.

"Once again, I win," Tyler said, beginning to count his wad of money.

I pushed my remaining dollars together without tallying them. "Here, you can have mine, too."

He looked surprised. "Don't you want to know how much you ended up with?"

"Not really," I said. "Money isn't everything."

He snorted humorously. "If you wanna win, it is!"

Saundra shook her head, smiling. "Okay, Tyler, I think a little humility would do well here."

He looked sheepish, like he'd been caught doing something dreadful. "Thanks for playing my game, girls."

"Any time," Andie replied, laughing.

"It was very enlightening," I said, helping to fold up the board and put away the little green houses and red hotels. It was obvious Saundra hadn't taught her son about the dangers of greed.

When the game lid was secure, I turned around to ask Daddy something, but he was sound asleep. His head had dropped down against his chest, and his hands were folded across his lap. "Looks like someone's had a rough day," I whispered to Saundra.

"Your father's a tired man." The gentle, motherly way she said it made me wonder even more.

Much later in the evening, Andie and I finally had a chance to have our little talk. Actually, it turned out to be a big deal. Much bigger than I ever dreamed. Andie had totally lost it over a chance encounter on the beach. And on the first day, no less!

10

I propped myself up with one elbow on the queen-sized bed in Andie's room, studying her as I lay on my side. I couldn't believe what I'd just heard. "Let me get this straight," I said. "Did you say you think this guy could be your future husband?"

Her eyes sparkled as she rolled over, staring goo-goo-eyed at the ceiling. "In my entire life, I've never met a guy like this. I mean, he's Hispanic, just like me."

I could see that Stan and Ryan had done a number on her back home. "Okay, so he and you are ethnically correct; so what?"

"Don't you see?" she said. "This could be the reason God let me catch the plane this morning."

She was turning irrational on me!

"You're kidding, right?" I looked at her. Then I sat up and peered down into her eyes. "Who are you, and what have you done with my best friend?"

She sat up, nearly knocking me over. "You're not funny, Holly. I'm serious. I want to get to know Rico while I'm here." She sighed, her eyes getting that dreamy, faraway look in them again. "Please don't say I shouldn't."

"Remember what our moms discussed about not pairing off?"

She shook her head. "This isn't like that. Rico's different."

Now I was really confused. "He's a *boy*, right?"

"Double duh . . ."

"But you hardly know him," I pointed out. "Besides, I bet he's not a Christian, is he?"

"We didn't talk about that." Her face looked glum for a moment, then it brightened. "I could witness to him and lead him to the Lord."

"That's risky," I said. "And while you're spending time talking to him about Christ, you're getting in over your head. It doesn't work that way."

I waited for a comeback, but she was silent. Finally I dealt with the real issue—the thing that was really bugging me. "I thought you were coming here to spend time with *me*," I said softly.

"Oh, Holly, we'll be spending lots of time together. Rico won't be able to come around every day. You'll see." She hugged me playfully. "You don't have to be jealous. No one could ever take your place."

After several more minutes of guy talk, I excused myself and headed to my own room. Andie had more than flipped; she'd completely lost her ability to reason.

I pulled out my journal and wrote my feelings about this first day at Daddy's. *Monday, July 11: I'm confused. Andie met a guy on the beach today. His name is Rico Hernandez. She thinks he's Mr. Wonderful, but I think her objectivity is totally out of whack.*

One minute she says maybe he's her future husband. Why? Just because he's Hispanic. Then she says maybe she's supposed to lead him to Christ—that's why she met him. And last, she thinks maybe this was the reason she got on the plane today. Like meeting Rico is somehow providential.

Whew! She's got her mission mixed up big-time. And short of locking her in her room, I have no idea what to do with her.

Andie's trying to convince me that he won't be hanging around all the time. But the way he looks at her . . . Well, I'll guess we'll find out soon enough.

I closed my journal, feeling dejected. Andie's mom had put her good faith in me. I couldn't let her—or Andie—down.

♥ ♥ ♥

The next day, after Tyler's summer math class, he convinced us to build a giant sand castle with him. Saundra had several errands to run after lunch, so I agreed to baby-sit. Since she was expecting a call from Daddy, I brought the portable phone out on the beach with us.

Tyler, Andie, and I were well into the blueprint planning when Rico showed up. At least he wasn't walking around here half naked, like yesterday. Today, he wore a sleeveless blue T-shirt over his bulging chest muscles and a pair of gray nylon surfer shorts. High on his left shoulder, he balanced two Boogie boards, steadying them with his super-tan hand.

"Cool castle," he said, acknowledging me with a nod of his head. But his gaze quickly found Andie's, and before I knew it, they were headed for the ocean.

"Who's he?" Tyler asked.

"Some guy," I said. "Ever see him around before?" *I hope he's not an illegal immigrant or something*, I thought, before Tyler could respond.

I probed some more. "Think hard . . . His name's Rico Hernandez."

Tyler packed the sand hard with his cupped hands. "I think Sean might know about him."

What was that supposed to mean?

I dropped the subject of Rico but asked Tyler about Sean Hamilton, the boy I'd met last Christmas when Carrie and I came to visit. "Does Sean still come over and hang out with you sometimes?"

"Sure," Tyler said, standing up and surveying his so-called moat. "He's over here a lot. Dad likes him."

"Really?"

"Yeah, we go to his church sometimes."

Fabulous news!

"You do?" I was dying to know if Saundra ever went along. "What about your mom; does she go, too?"

"Nah, Mom's not into church much. I'm not exactly sure why."

I wished he had said she went at least occasionally, but then, I guess I could understand why Saundra wouldn't want to. Church, after all, was worship. Freely giving of our love and praise to God. Since she didn't believe in a personal God, she would probably find worship rather tedious. I determined in my heart to pray more often for the new Mrs. Meredith.

The castle was nearing completion when Andie and her possible future husband came racing out of the water and onto the beach. He'd taken his shirt off and was chasing her. He looked intent upon *catching* her, too. They ran down the beach and out of sight.

I sighed, frustrated. Andie was making it hard for me to watch over her. Besides, her mom would be very upset if she knew what was going on.

I tried to focus my attention on my young charge, who seemed eager to finish his castle before suppertime. Since I didn't want to abandon Tyler and possibly spoil things between Saundra and me—I wanted to show as much responsibility as I could—I tried to forget about Andie and Rico.

More shouts drifted to my ears. Then there was a long silence, followed by giggling. Andie's giggles!

I raced to the grassy mound a few yards from Tyler's castle, peering into the distance. The heat of the midday sun beat against my shoulders, and I shielded my eyes from the glare.

My father's beachfront property was rather small compared to his sprawling house. I could see Andie and Rico sitting on a boulder overlooking the ocean, and judging by the distance, they were probably trespassing on someone's property.

Just then the phone rang. I hurried back to the beach blanket and grabbed it. Pressing the On button, I said, "Hello, Meredith residence."

"Is this Holly?"

"Yes, it is."

"This is Rosita Martinez. How's everything there?"

Oh, great, she probably wants to talk to Andie.

My heart was pounding. "We're having a great time," I said, trying to remain calm.

"Is Andrea nearby? I'd like to talk with her."

I gulped. There was no way Andie would ever hear me calling this far away. "I'm sorry, Andie can't come to the phone right now," I managed to squeak out.

"Oh, she's tired? Bless her heart."

I didn't want to lie. Mrs. Martinez thought Andie was taking a nap.

"May I have her call you later?" Smart move. This would buy me some time.

"No, no," she insisted. "I'll call her back in about an hour."

"Okay, I'll tell her. Good-bye." I zapped the Off button and flung the phone back on the beach blanket.

Tyler noticed my anger. "What's wrong?"

"Stay here; I'll be right back." I stormed down the beach, avoiding the tide foam as it crept close to my bare toes. "How dare Andie put me in this situation," I whispered, feeling the anger rise in my face.

I could see the cozy twosome half-snuggling on the giant boulder. Well, they weren't really touching, but their shoulders seemed somewhat connected. When I reached yelling distance, I held my hands up to my mouth and shouted her name.

Andie turned to look.

Good. I'd gotten her attention. Now I was too stubborn to holler out the message. Instead, I motioned to her with my hand, making large round motions over and over until I was sure she would catch on. But she didn't respond instantly, as I'd hoped. And I was too angry to stand there and wait for her. Turning back, I headed into the salty wind.

Tyler wanted to do an inspection of his castle creation with me. We began our ritual. He stood guard on one side while I recited the names of the towers and gables and things. He'd written everything down for me. Then we traded, and I was the guard and he did the same on the back side of the masterpiece.

Minutes had passed since I'd called to Andie. I was beside myself because she hadn't come. No way I was going back down and calling for her again. I refused to cater to her obvious game playing.

I wanted to run inside and check the clock. Andie's mom had said she'd call back in an hour. This was treacherous. I hated being caught in the middle like this.

"You want a snack or something?" I asked Tyler.

"Sure." We headed toward the house.

While Tyler poured lemonade for both of us, I stood out on the deck overlooking the beach to the south. Two specks of humanity sat suspended in space and time on the same large rock as before. What was so important that Andie hadn't responded and come as I'd requested? Was she talking to Rico about God? Was *that* it?

I wished I had some binoculars. Then I remembered Tyler's telescope. He'd set it up on a tripod in one of the guest rooms last Christmas when Carrie and I were here. "Do you still have your telescope?" I asked when I went back inside.

Tyler handed me a glass of lemonade. "Sure, wanna have a look?"

As it turned out, the "spy tube" was set up in Tyler's bedroom, just down the hallway on the main level. He helped me get it focused, and I purposely aimed it toward the ocean so he wouldn't know what I was doing and spill the beans to Andie later.

"I'll be right back," he said, running out of the room. Just the break I needed.

Quickly, I moved the long black tube in the southern-most direction. There they were—Andie and Rico. I focused again, pulling them in closer.

Yikes! Rico was holding Andie's hand. And by the look on his face, their conversation had nothing to do with God. Nothing at all.

I thought about the promise I'd made to Andie last night. How loyal should I be if it meant lying to cover for her?

"Dear Lord," I whispered, still looking through the telescope. "Please help me do the right thing."

11

I headed back to the kitchen, remembering to check the clock. Nearly four-thirty! It was an hour later in Dressel Hills. Andie's dad was probably home with the twins, giving her mom a chance to chat in peace. Now, if I could just get Andie to be here when her mother called back.

An idea struck me just then. I waited for Tyler to finish washing his hands, then the two of us went back down to the beach. I knelt on the beach blanket in front of the radio and scanned the tuner, hunting for a Christian station. When I found a contemporary one, I told Tyler to cover his ears. "Let's crank up the music." He nodded, smiling, and I turned up the volume all the way.

Marching down the beach a short distance, I checked to see if Andie had heard. Yep! She was getting up and heading this way. And not surprisingly, Rico was tagging along beside her, holding her hand.

"It worked," I muttered to myself, heading back to turn the music down—just a tad. I wanted the contemporary Christian music to be playing when they arrived.

Tyler and I fitted a drawbridge for his castle while I waited for Andie's return. Without turning to look, I knew they were back by the sound of Andie's laughter.

Rico came over to check out Tyler's creation. "Incredible," he said.

Andie followed close behind. "Wow, Tyler, you're good."

Tyler grinned, obviously proud. "Thanks, but Holly did a lot of it, too."

I wondered how long before Andie would notice the Christian music or if she'd even comment about it. She avoided my eyes as she sat down on the beach blanket, brushing the sand off and smoothing the wrinkles. Rico sat beside her and reached for the radio. "Anybody listening to this?" he asked me.

"Tyler and I are," I said.

"Okay, then. No problem." He set the radio back down on the blanket, the music still going strong. "Sorry."

I don't know why I was surprised that he was polite about it. Sitting on the edge of the blanket, I held up the portable phone. "Your mom called while you were gone," I told Andie.

Her eyes bugged out. "She did?"

"Uh-huh. And she'll be calling back any minute."

Andie glanced at Rico. Her face turned a little pale. "What did you tell her?"

"Nothing. She thought you were napping."

Andie burst out laughing. "You said that?"

"No. It didn't happen like that." I turned away, hoping she'd drop the subject.

Then the phone rang. I held my breath, hoping it was Daddy, which it was.

"Hi, Holly. Having fun?"

"Sure am," I said. "But it would be lots more fun if you were here."

He didn't comment on that, instead he asked to speak to Saundra.

"She's out running errands. *I'm* in charge of the house."

"Holding down the fort, eh?" His chuckle disguised the

tiredness in his voice, but only for a second. "Well, when Saundra returns, tell her I'll be a little late tonight. She'll know what that means."

I drew in a deep breath. "Everything okay at work?"

"Oh, work's not a problem," he said.

Something else was?

"Tell her not to wait for supper," he continued. I heard the heaviness in his voice. "I'll pick up something on my way home."

"Okay, Daddy," I said, wondering what was so important to keep him late. Again. I was starting to feel like he was an absentee person around here. Just like Andie.

Discouraged, I turned the phone off. Something seemed wrong. I couldn't overlook the obvious sigh in Daddy's voice.

When the phone rang again several minutes later, Andie and Rico were still flirting.

I reached for the phone. "Meredith residence, Holly speaking."

"Hello, Holly, it's Rosita again." Andie's mom!

"Uh, just a minute." I pointed to the phone, motioning for Andie.

She shook her head, waving her hands as though to say she wasn't there and had no intention of talking.

I frowned, covering the mouthpiece. "It's your mom."

She stood up and said, "I just talked to her last night," and walked away.

Andie was taking this way too far. I wanted to shout at her, make it obvious to her mom that Andie was right here— let Mrs. Martinez know she was pulling her spoiled brat routine. But I didn't dare. After all, I'd been the one who'd begged to have Andie come along.

Giving up, I uncovered the mouthpiece. "Uh, hello?"

"Yes?"

"I'm sorry, Mrs. Martinez, Andie still can't come to the phone." I swallowed hard, wishing Andie would get over here and take her call. It was her mother on the line, for pete's sake.

"She isn't ill, is she?"

Depending how you looked at it, sick was definitely a possibility. I watched Andie run into the ocean with Rico and the Boogie boards.

"Holly, are you there?" Mrs. Martinez sounded concerned.

"Uh . . . yes, I'm sorry."

"Did Andrea get airsick on the plane?"

"Oh, no, she didn't have any trouble flying," I said, grasping at straws. "But . . . she hasn't been herself lately."

"Well, I hope Andrea's getting plenty of rest and watching the junk food." She paused. "You girls aren't staying up all hours, are you?"

I laughed. "My stepmom would never allow that."

"That's good." She seemed satisfied to hear that. "Well, I want Andrea to call me when she feels better. Have her use her phone card."

"Okay. Good-bye." It was all I could do to control my actions this time as I turned the phone off.

Andie saw that it was safe to come back, but I was too furious to look at her. I called to Tyler, "Come on, kiddo. Let's get cleaned up for supper."

Between the two of us, Tyler and I gathered up the beach blanket, his castle-making equipment and radio, and the phone. Without a glance back, we headed to the house, leaving Andie with her precious Rico.

♥   ♥   ♥

I was in the shower when Tyler started pounding on the bathroom door. "Holly! Someone's on the phone for you."

I turned the water off for a second. "Who is it?"

"Sean Hamilton," he said. "Should I tell him to call you back later?"

"That'll be fine. Thanks." I finished soaping up, then rinsed off, wondering about Sean. If he wanted to see me, I'd have to make it perfectly clear that I wasn't interested in anything but friendship.

After dressing, I towel-dried my hair and fluffed it with my fingers. I stood in front of the mirror, holding the long strands out. Andie was forever teasing me about getting my hair cut, but the way I figured, if I ever *did* decide to cut it, and then if I hated it, I'd be stuck with it for a very long time. Whew, I couldn't begin to imagine how many years it would take to grow my hair this long again.

Still, the washing and drying thing was a pain sometimes. Especially in humid weather like this. In order to hurry up the drying process so I could braid it before supper, I pushed the sliding glass door open and stepped out onto my private balcony overlooking the ocean.

That's when I spotted Andie with Rico, standing side by side in the shallow ocean tide, facing into the sun. He had his arm draped around her shoulder, and she leaned her head against his arm. If I hadn't been so upset with her, I might've thought they looked sweet together out there.

But anger welled up inside me, and I clenched my teeth. Nope, I wouldn't even begin to give credence to her tender moment. I turned on my heels and flew into the house.

♥   ♥   ♥

Sean did call back later. Much later. The phone rang as Andie and I helped Saundra clean up the kitchen. Tyler got the phone, and a big smile stretched across his face when he announced that it was Sean.

I excused myself. "Hey," I said.

"Welcome to Southern California," came the deep voice.

"Thanks, it's nice to be here."

"How long this time?"

"Two weeks," I replied. "Long enough to get a decent tan. Maybe."

"Tans are way overrated," he teased.

I chuckled. "Don't I know."

"Well, I was wondering if I could see you sometime while you're here." He paused for a moment, sounding a little unsure of himself. "Maybe we could take that walk on the beach after all."

I wanted to set some ground rules right away, but when you're standing in the kitchen with several pairs of ears listening in, it's not so easy.

"That'd be fun," I said, thinking that I would explain my decision about guys when we walked together.

"How does tomorrow after lunch sound?" Sean asked, sounding more confident.

"That'll work." I bit my lip, hoping I was doing the right thing.

"Okay, I'll see you then." And he hung up.

Walking in broad daylight on the beach with Sean Hamilton couldn't be classified as a real date. Besides, I knew my mother would approve because he was a Christian. And she'd met Sean last April when he and Daddy came to Dressel Hills to ski. She had wanted to be introduced to him formally right there at the ski lodge. At the time it seemed sort of awkward, but now it made good sense. Caring parents were like that—wanting only the best for their kids.

So why was *Andie* fighting against her parents' wishes?

12

I went outside and sat on the deck, waiting for Daddy to show up while Saundra was in the living room entertaining a neighbor lady. Tyler had run back to the beach to check on his sand castle.

I was beginning to wonder where Andie was, when she showed up in a long, white caftan, ready for a relaxing evening.

"Look, Holly, I know you're mad, but could you at least tell me what my mom called about?" Andie stood there, hands on hips, waiting for my answer.

I set my soda down deliberately on the wicker table next to me. "Well, it's about time. I thought you'd never ask."

"So?"

"Your mom wants you to call her back." There. Now let's see what Andie did with that tidbit of information.

"Did you tell her about Rico?" she asked, almost sheepishly.

"Of course I didn't." I leaped off the chaise. "Does this look like the face of a friend you can't trust? Does it?"

Her eyes suddenly seemed sad. "What *did* you say to my mom?"

"That you're breaking every one of her rules. That you're

going crazy out here; you're totally out of control. And if you don't get your act together, I'm shipping you home on the very next plane." I studied her as I eased myself back down into the lounge chair. "Is that what you wanted me to say?"

Andie sat down. "Is that how you feel? That you want me to go home?"

I inhaled and held my breath for a moment. "Well, I think it might be a good idea, especially if you're going to lose your head over a guy who can't get a date with girls his own age."

"Holly!"

"C'mon, Andie, face it. You're only fourteen. What could he possibly want with a girl your age?"

"You don't even know Rico." She folded her arms. "Listen, I don't want to hurt your feelings. Is that what this is about? Are you mad because we're not doing very much together?"

Sure, that was part of it, but I was tired of taking the rap for the rift between us. Jealousy was becoming less and less of an issue. I'd seen the lusty look in Rico's eyes. "Don't you remember the lunch we had at the Soda Straw, all of us together? What was the point of telling your mom you were going to follow her rules when the minute you get out of her sight, you go nuts?"

"Okay," she agreed. "I need a break. What am I doing that's so bad? I mean, we've all been together . . . most of the time. And nobody's dating or anything, not really." Her face was red and angry. She was fighting too hard for Rico.

I looked away, letting my eyes roam over the beach to the boulder where she had sat with Rico. "You're in way over your head, Andie," I said without looking at her. "If you have any sense, you'll cool it."

"You're getting preachy."

I sighed. "I'm sure you've heard this stuff many times from your mom, at church, from our youth pastor."

She looked at me like I was from some other planet. "Holly, save your voice," she said. "We're not doing anything wrong."

"Maybe not yet, but things lead to, you know, other things." I was having a hard time getting this out. "You can't fool around physically without getting hurt . . . eventually."

"I can't believe you're saying this," she said, standing up. "Everything's under control with Rico, if that's what you mean." She walked to the sliding door. "I have to make a phone call." Picking up the long skirt of her caftan, she stepped inside and slid the glass door shut.

Reaching for my soda, I thought of the stress I'd endured back home with Carrie and Stephie constantly in my face— how I couldn't wait to get away from them. Away from their snooping. Away from Stan and his constant stupidity.

Peace and quiet—what a joke. So far, the past two days had been nothing short of total chaos. How ignorant of me to think I was finally going to have a real vacation.

♥   ♥   ♥

The word *stress* hung in my mind as I tiptoed inside and hurried downstairs to my room. I found my journal and began to pour some of the tension onto the lines of the notebook paper.

Tuesday, July 12: I think Andie and her friend Rico are not only freaking me out, they're turning me into a watchdog. Tonight when I talked to Andie about her spending time with him, I honestly sounded like somebody's mother! I hate this role, yet I agreed to take it. In a way, it's Andie's mom's fault for asking me to "watch over" her daughter. I'm turning into something I don't like.

If Andie would take more responsibility for herself, I could relax. Relax. Hmm, that's something I think my dad oughta do, too. He sounded so exhausted when he called from the office this afternoon. Here it is already 8:30, and he's still not home.

I'm beginning to worry. And I don't think I'm the only one. Saundra isn't herself. I can see it in her eyes. She's worried, too.

After I finished writing, I knelt down and began to pray for Saundra. And for Daddy. Then I felt compelled to pray for Saundra's salvation. "Make her want to know you," I told the Lord. "And let me be more open to her during this visit. In Jesus' name, amen."

I was surprised how quickly the time had passed. It was nearly dark outside when I stood up. I reached for the emerald lamp on the oak table next to the bed. Turning it on, I sat there on the floor in the stillness of my empty room, reveling in God's peace.

The quiet moments spent there were the calm before the hurricane. When I went back upstairs, I didn't really mean to eavesdrop, but as I was turning into the kitchen, I heard Saundra talking to her neighbor lady. It sounded as if they were standing at the door, saying good-bye to each other. "Do take care of that husband of yours," her friend said.

"Doing my best," Saundra answered. "But he's not slowing down enough, I'm sorry to say." I heard her sniffle. "I'll know more when Robert gets home later."

I strained to hear. Saundra was saying that Daddy had to stop and get some lab results. I held my breath, afraid to breathe. So *that's* why he'd called this afternoon.

I didn't like the sound of this. When Saundra came into the kitchen, I stuck my head in the fridge, pretending to look for something to eat.

"Hungry already?" she asked.

Slowly, I withdrew from the refrigerator. "Not really," I whispered.

"What is it, dear?" She put her hand under my chin and lifted my face to meet her gaze. "What's wrong?"

"I heard what you were saying just now," I muttered, tears

coming fast. "What's wrong with Daddy?"

"Oh, that." She waved her hand as though there was nothing in the world to worry about. "Your father's a work-aholic, that's all. His doctor wants him to slow down, but—" she sighed—"you know how your father is."

"So he's not sick, then?"

She pondered the thought. "I think he's a little stressed, that's all."

I honestly didn't believe her. The answers she'd given sounded like white lies to me. Which made me even more concerned. What was she hiding?

♥   ♥   ♥

The next day was Wednesday. Daddy stayed home from work, which was fabulous. He lounged around in his silk pajamas and robe most of the morning. Maybe he and I would have a chance to talk. Maybe not an intimate heart-to-heart talk, but a good, solid one would do.

We sat outside on the deck, where Saundra served Andie, Tyler, and me a breakfast of bacon and eggs. Dad got granola and an orange without his usual coffee. My stepmom played the energetic hostess, rushing in and out of the house, bringing more platters of jelly toast and bacon.

Tyler seemed to enjoy himself, chattering on and on about the sand creations he was planning to make.

"What are *your* plans today?" Daddy asked me, including both Andie and me in his gaze.

"Sean and I are going for a walk after lunch."

Andie jumped on that statement. "Sean Hamilton's coming over? You mean I finally get to meet him?" She was too eager. Or maybe she didn't really care at all about meeting Sean. In her mind, maybe my having a guy around would get her off the hook with me about Rico.

Before I could answer her, Daddy spoke up. "That Sean . . . he's really terrific." He smiled, leaning back in the sun, like he was remembering a fond moment. "I can't think of a nicer fellow for my daughter to be seeing."

"Daddy!" I blushed. "I'm not seeing anyone. I'm too young to date, remember?"

"Oh, sure," he said. "But if you ever decide to do such a thing, well, Sean's my first choice."

Andie's eyes danced with glee. She was obviously delighted that the subject of boys had come up.

Then I did something I'd probably live to regret. I asked Daddy about Rico Hernandez. "Do you know him?"

Andie's eyes shot warning signals.

"Rico, you say?" He shielded his eyes from the sun. "Now, there's an interesting kid." He didn't say Rico was a *good* kid.

Andie must have read more into his statement, though, because she sat up straight in her chair, sporting a huge grin.

"So you know Rico?" I asked.

"I certainly do," Daddy responded, holding his glass up for more ice water. Saundra hopped to it and got him some fresh water. "Rico lives up the beach. I've known his family for a number of years; in fact, his dad's a brilliant doctor—one of mine."

Andie's eyes did a complete flip.

"What kind of doctor?" I asked, but Saundra didn't give Daddy time to answer. Instantly, she changed the subject.

Exactly what was she hiding?

13

My walk with Sean that afternoon took us several miles down the beach. Tropical palm trees dotted the bluffs jutting high above the coastline, making the encounter seem all the more exotic.

"I was going to send you an email before you came," he said cautiously, "but the timing didn't seem quite right." His light blond hair rippled in the breeze. "I've been thinking about you, Holly."

I swallowed. This wasn't supposed to happen. "Look, Sean," I said, thinking now was as good a time as any to lay down my ground rules, "I wanted to tell you on the phone about something, but it was—" I paused—"shall we say, inconvenient at the time."

Sean looked puzzled.

I continued. "Last month, after church camp, I came to the conclusion that I wasn't happy with the way things were going for me with boys. I mean, I don't have a problem with being friends or anything."

Sean nodded enthusiastically, like he could see my point one hundred percent.

"I won't be fifteen for another seven months, and it's not really the age thing so much as the pressure of most boy-girl relationships. Know what I mean?"

He said he did.

"So, for that reason, I'm going to level with you. I don't want to hurt your feelings, but I'm not interested in dating while I'm here. Besides, my mom wouldn't approve anyway."

"That's cool."

We found seashells at the high-tide line, packed close together in the sand, as we walked leisurely toward Daddy's house. Sean was nice enough to fill his pants pockets with my beach souvenirs. He told me about the secondhand car his folks were helping him buy and his summer job at a Christian radio station.

"Sounds like fun," I said. "Do you want to become a disc jockey after high school?"

"Nah, it's just one of my hobbies." He ran his fingers through his short, thick hair. "I'm thinking more about going to med school, though."

This was news to me. "What kind of medicine?"

He turned to look at me, smiling. "For as long as I can remember, I've been interested in hearts." His smile broadened. "I'm not talking Holly-Heart here, so relax, okay? But ever since sixth grade when Dr. Hernandez came to school for Professional Day, I've thought about being a cardiologist."

Dr. Hernandez . . . a heart doctor?

"Rico's dad's a cardiologist?" I blurted.

He nodded. "So . . . you've met Rico?"

"Well, actually, he's Andie's friend," I said quickly.

"Rico's a little old for her, don't you think?"

I could hardly make sense of things—my brain was clouded with the fact that Daddy's heart needed help. That's why Saundra had been covering for him. She didn't want to worry me. Daddy's heart . . . what could be wrong?

I wasn't doing very well carrying my end of the conversation. "I'm sorry, what?"

Sean repeated himself. "Rico's been out of high school for

a year. He ought to be dating girls his age."

"No kidding!"

"Does Andie know he's not a Christian?" he asked.

"Well, she says she wants to witness to him," I explained, letting Sean know in no uncertain terms that I was opposed to their friendship. "It's kinda touchy, though, because Andie had problems with a couple of guys back home. They, well . . . *one* of them made fun of her for being Hispanic, and because of that I think she's more vulnerable to Rico right now."

Sean nodded. "Prejudice is widespread around here. It's everywhere, really." He seemed to understand my concern for Andie, too, and I felt instantly better for having confided in him.

♥　♥　♥

Daddy seemed more relaxed when I arrived home. He was sitting in his study reading a poem to Andie. She sat across from him in a comfortably cool leather chair. Rich, gleaming cherrywood bookshelves shone against the sunlight streaming in from the skylight above.

I tiptoed in, standing silently as he read. When the poem was finished, Andie applauded. "You never told me your father writes poetry," she said, observing me.

"He does?" I came around, leaning over his chair. "You do?"

He held up the printed pages. The title, "A Year to Celebrate," made my heart glad. It must have been inspired by his newfound joy. Daddy had become a Christian last April.

"You wrote this?" I walked slowly around his chair, scanning the lines on the page. It was free verse, beautifully flowing with a loose rhyming pattern.

"Well, what do you think?" His eyes searched mine.

"It's fabulous!"

Andie agreed. "You get your writing talent from your dad, Holly."

Daddy's eyes shone. He reached for a pencil and began scribbling on the back of his paper.

I walked around his large study, stopping to inspect the gold-framed family pictures on his enormous desk. Baby pictures. One of me wearing a red Valentine dress with white lace edging, one of Carrie cuddling a white bunny with pink ears.

Andie wandered over, looking at the pictures. "Aw, how sweet. Holly, you were such a doll."

"Look how light my hair was then," I said. It looked the color of real butter—almost white.

"And it was so short and wispy," she said. We looked at Carrie's picture together. The resemblance between us was uncanny, even as babies. "You could pass as identical twins," Andie said.

"Yeah, born four years apart."

Saundra poked her head in the door. "Anybody ready for tea?"

Andie looked at me, surprised. "Tea?"

Daddy chuckled. "Yes, we have afternoon tea around here every so often. Saundra's quite a hostess." He smiled proudly, and Saundra came over and laid a big smacker right on his lips.

I chose peppermint tea with honey, because that's probably what Mom was drinking back home right about now. I honestly missed her and wished I could confide in her about Andie's shenanigans. Unfortunately I'd promised to keep my friend's private life a secret.

After we pigged out on finger pastries and a variety of other sweet cakes, I thanked Saundra and asked Daddy if we could talk alone.

"Not now," Saundra said, standing up suddenly as though she'd forgotten something important.

"Time for my pills," Daddy said, apologizing for her. "We'll talk later, okay?"

I went over and kissed his cheek. "I'll be waiting."

Daddy smiled faintly, leaning his head back against the padded leather. "I don't think I can stand having two doting women in the same house."

I blew a kiss, wishing Saundra hadn't cut me off like that. Something must have shown up on those lab tests for Daddy to be staying home all day. Worried, I headed down the stairs with Andie trailing behind.

"Your mom called while you were out with Sean," Andie said, following me into my room.

"She did? When?"

"Right after you left."

"Why didn't Daddy say something?" I asked.

"Because he was asleep and Saundra was next door."

"So *you* answered the phone?" I couldn't believe this. Andie was certainly making herself at home here.

"Well, I kinda thought it might be Rico," she admitted softly. "That's why."

"What would *he* want?"

"Oh, nothing much," she said, but I wondered if they weren't making plans for later.

"Well, what did Mom say?"

Andie grinned. "She wanted to talk to you, what else?"

"What did you say?"

"That you were out with some boy, sneaking off with him into the night."

"You did not."

"Bet me." Her face looked serious, and she wasn't twisting her hair like she usually did at a time like this. Was she fibbing me? Or . . . was she trying to get back at me for my reaction to Rico?

"Your mom said you'd have to come home immediately." Andie's face was severely serious now.

"Andie, come on!" I wailed.

Her face broke into a spiteful grin. "How's it feel?"

I lashed out. "That's not fair. You lied."

"And you didn't?" She looked absolutely haughty. "Well, now we're even."

Even or not, I didn't like it one bit. I flew out of the room and upstairs to call my mom.

14

The next morning, bright and early, I slipped out of bed and found my journal. *Thursday, July 14: Andie and I aren't getting along so well. I wish she'd drop Rico flat, but even after we talked late last night, she seemed more determined than ever to ignore me and do things her way. Shoot, she's not just being stubborn, she's outright defiant! Andie's acting really different here. I can't remember her being so rebellious back home.*

That bizarre comment she said she made to my mom about me sneaking off into the night with Sean . . . Where did that come from? If I didn't know and trust Andie the way I do, I'd think she was planning something like that herself.

Whew—Mom sounded depressed when I called last night. She said Stan was giving Uncle Jack fits over his new curfew—guess he's been staying out too late, breaking house rules. I told her I thought Ryan Davis was a bad influence on him. She agrees.

Mom thinks my coming out here might be just the thing my little sister needed to make her appreciate me more. She said Carrie actually misses me. Stephie, too.

Well . . . Daddy and I didn't get to have our talk, at least not yesterday. It seems like every time there's the slightest window of opportunity, Saundra shows up and slams it shut. I don't know what her problem is, but she's starting to drive me crazy. I have a right to know what's wrong with my father. And if she's going to keep being so secretive, well, I guess I'll just have to confront her.

I showered, dressed, and wandered onto my balcony. In the distance I could see a tall blonde jogger on the beach with a black dog. I was sure it was Sean Hamilton and his Labrador dog, Sunshine.

I thought about our talk yesterday. Sean's face had shown his approval for what I'd said . . . and his words seemed to agree. But I had a funny feeling he was going along with my decision to appease me. Sometimes it was hard to read Sean. I wished I had a better handle on things—on how he really felt.

Tyler was more hyper than usual at breakfast. We ate at the breakfast nook, and Andie came dragging in late. She looked exhausted, like she hadn't slept all night. I played with the tan linen napkin under my fork. Still observing Andie, I listened halfheartedly as Tyler chattered about tomorrow's trip to Universal Studios in Hollywood.

"I can't wait to ride through the earthquake on the back lot," he said as Saundra finally came around and sat at the head of the table. "Power cables snapping and sparking with electricity, train wrecks, lethal fumes, and a sixty-thousand-gallon tidal wave coming right at us!"

"Cool," Andie said sleepily, her curls drooping as she tugged on her bathrobe.

I wondered why Saundra was sitting in Daddy's place. "Did Daddy go to work today?" I asked, watching for signs of him.

Saundra began passing a platter of pancakes around. "Since your father is taking off tomorrow, he had to go in to the office early today." She volunteered nothing else. Zero info . . . zilch!

I breathed deeply, surveying the situation. Her eyes refused to meet mine. But I watched her anyway. I *had* to know. "Is he okay?"

Saundra nodded, still avoiding my persistent gaze. Then Tyler launched into his excited chatter about King Kong, Animal Planet Live, and the Rugrats Magic Adventure, along with everything else we were going to see and do tomorrow, and Saundra actually seemed relieved.

So . . . was that how she wanted to play this game? Just ignore me? Say whatever she pleased to get me off her back?

I was freaked out, and even more so when it came time to eat and no one said grace. "Excuse me?" I glared at Tyler. "Didn't we forget something?"

"Oh, sorry." He passed the pancake syrup to me.

"That's *not* what I meant."

Andie came to my rescue. "Somebody pray," she muttered, leaning her mop of curls into her hands.

"I will." And I did.

When I was finished, I noticed that Saundra had bowed her head right along with the rest of us. A first.

I spread butter and syrup on my warm pancakes and began to chow down.

After breakfast, Andie went back to bed. She said she hadn't slept well last night. I really wasn't interested in her sleep patterns, so I headed to my room to straighten things up and have my devotions.

Later, I went upstairs to see if I could help Saundra with anything. "That's very thoughtful of you, dear," she said, "but the cleaning lady will be coming tomorrow morning. The best thing for you to do is to have your room picked up a bit before she comes."

"It's nice and neat," I said, dying to broach the subject of Daddy's health. But she looked rather busy as she sat at her desk in the kitchen alcove, scanning her daily planner.

Glancing up, she said, "Since Tyler's going to be busy at summer school, how would you and Andie like to go to lunch with me?"

"Okay."

"We could go to Marcie's first and have our nails done. Would you like that?"

"Marcie's?"

"Oh, you'll adore the place," she said, all bubbly. "Marcie's is the most exclusive beauty salon in Beverly Hills. We'll get all dressed up and go, okay, dear?"

"Sure," I said, but getting all prissy wasn't my thing. Having a manicure was okay, but fake nails and colored nail polish? Ick!

In a flash, Saundra picked up the phone and made lunch reservations at some exotic place in Beverly Hills.

I hurried downstairs to inform Andie.

Tiptoeing into her room, I whispered, "Andie."

She was sound asleep.

"Hey, wake up, we're going somewhere really fabulous for lunch."

No response. She was out cold.

I shrugged and turned to go back upstairs. Saundra was talking on the phone when I showed up in the kitchen again. I waited till she was finished, then explained that Andie hadn't slept much last night. "Maybe we should wait awhile and let her rest."

Saundra's eyebrows shot up. "How long do you think she should sleep?"

I glanced at the gold-and-black clock on the wall. "It's already nine-thirty. When's our nail appointment?"

"Eleven on the dot." Saundra went back to her daily planner. I noticed several mini-lists inside. She and I had *something* in common. Maybe it was a starting place.

"I make lists, too," I began, a little cautious at first. "I have a whole notebook full of lists."

"That's nice, dear," she said, not really paying attention.

I took a deep breath now. "One of my favorite lists is my prayer list."

She looked up quickly.

"It helps me keep track of the people I'm praying for."

"You certainly sound organized." Her comment was a bit patronizing.

"Well, it sure helps . . . especially when the Lord answers my prayers. Then I check off my list with the date of the answer."

Saundra had a quizzical expression on her face. "Your father started doing something similar to that recently."

"Daddy? Really?"

"Yes, he's quite taken with the Bible and church and such things."

"That's really great, don't you think?"

"Well, I try to steer clear of his current obsession," she said, making it sound like Daddy's interest in spiritual things was merely a passing fancy.

"You'd be surprised how the Lord can help you, especially when things go bad. Like Daddy's health, for instance."

She frowned. "What makes you think your father's health is bad?"

"Well, if Rico's father is a cardiologist, and he's one of Daddy's doctors—"

"Well," she snapped, "your father has seen Dr. Hernandez only one time. So I don't think you can jump to any conclusions."

"That's just it," I said softly. "I don't want to jump to conclusions. I want the straight truth."

She tapped her nails on the desk, studying me. And for a split second I wondered why she needed to have her nails redone. They were perfect. "Holly," she began, looking at me with sincere eyes. The tension between us felt white-hot. "Do you think I've been lying to you about your father?"

I sighed. "Well, I hope you're not trying to keep me in the dark. Maybe you're just protecting me, not really lying to me." Whew, I'd said it. Now it was her turn. Would she keep fibbing or was the truth about to emerge at last?

"You're a perceptive young lady," she said, throwing me for a loop. I honestly thought she'd continue her charade. "What would you like to know?"

Bracing myself against the possibility of bad news, I said, "I want to know what's wrong with Daddy."

"Let me see if I can explain this to you." She crossed her legs, smoothing her long voile skirt. "Your father's heart, along with suffering severe stress from having a minor heart attack about two years ago—"

I interrupted her. "Two years ago? Why didn't anyone tell me?"

She looked at the ceiling, like she was trying to get a grasp of things. "It was around the time of his sister's cancer diagnosis."

"Aunt Marla? She found out about her cancer in January—two and a half years ago."

"Yes, that's when your father had some trouble." She shook her head. "He started slowing down a bit. Remember when we drove over to that pretty little chapel to hear you sing with your youth choir?"

I nodded. "So, was Daddy's heart damaged back then? He seemed just fine to me."

"The heart attack was so slight, but it was enough to make him want to improve his diet and include more daily exercise. But as time went on, he got caught up in his hectic routine again."

"Does he follow a strict diet now?"

She ran her fingers through the length of her hair. "I'm doing my best to keep him on a low-fat diet. But he gets very little exercise, which isn't good, and he's so driven it's hard to get him to take time off. That's one of the reasons I was thrilled you were coming."

"Does he really have to work such long hours?" I asked.

She shook her head. "He's entirely his own boss, but that doesn't change his tendency to overwork."

"Can't you make him slow down?"

She smiled wistfully. "That would be nice."

"Well, maybe if I talk to—"

"No," she interrupted. "I don't want you to say anything about this to your father. He doesn't need the additional stress. And maybe if he thought you knew, he might be concerned that you'd be worried." She smiled a sweet, comforting smile. "You know how that goes."

It was obvious she knew Daddy well. But I wondered how his recent conversion to Christianity had affected their relationship. From listening to her, I could see there wasn't any change for the worse. That was good, because it sounded like Daddy needed someone very supportive now.

My next question was about his lab results. But I wasn't able to ask because the phone rang. Saundra caught it on the second ring.

"Meredith residence." A short pause. Then, "Yes, Andie's here, but she's resting." Saundra turned to me, covering the mouthpiece. "It's Rico Hernandez; he asked to speak to you."

"Me?"

What did Andie's boyfriend want with me?

15

"*Hello?*"

"Yeah, Holly, this is Rico. I thought you and Andie might wanna know about my beach party tomorrow night."

"Oh? What's the occasion?"

"Just some people getting together for a good time."

"What people?" I sounded like an interrogator, but I didn't care. I wanted to make things tough for him.

"Some of my college friends will be hangin' out, you know, just a bunch of kids."

Yeah, right. Sounded like a party I couldn't wait to miss!

"Andie and I have other plans," I said quickly. "Sorry. Bye." I was getting ready to hang up.

"Uh, wait, Holly. Is Andie doing okay?"

"Why wouldn't she be?"

"Well, uh, oh, nothing. Just tell her I said hi, and I'll see you two later."

See us later? Hadn't he listened? And why was he asking about Andie as though she were sick or something?

I dashed downstairs. "Andie, wake up!" She moaned and groaned when I shook her awake. "C'mon, sleeping beauty. My stepmom's got some great plans for us."

"I'm sleeping," she said, her throat raspy.

"You'd better shake a leg if you wanna go with us to Marcie's." I told her it was some expensive salon in Beverly Hills.

She carried on like she was too tired. "Do I have to go?"

"You'll be fine once you wake up," I assured her, now playfully pulling on the covers.

"Holly, I'm tired," she snapped at me. "Leave me alone."

I stood back, surveying the rumpled pile of covers billowing around her. "Are you kidding, you actually want to miss this?"

"I'm telling you to just go without me. I'll stay home and sleep. Have fun with your wicked stepmother." With that, she rolled over.

"Okay, have it your way." I left the room, purposely keeping the beach party invitation a secret. Closing the door behind me, I wondered how fast Andie would have snapped to it if I had mentioned Rico's party.

♥   ♥   ♥

Saundra and I did the town, all right. I managed to get by without having long, fakey nails, though. Just getting my cuticles soaked, pushed back, and trimmed was enough for me. After my nails were filed and shaped properly, I chose a pale pink polish that matched my shirt.

Several hair stylists went a little over the edge about my hair—especially the color and the length. No matter where I went, my hair seemed to attract people.

Afterward, Saundra and I headed for lunch in another posh area of Beverly Hills. During the drive there, and later after ordering our entree, I tried several times unsuccessfully to return to our former conversation about Daddy. I was still curious about the lab results, but Saundra was talkative about other things. Mostly the travel plans she was secretly making for their wedding anniversary in August.

"I tell you, Holly, your father is going to be so surprised." She looked happier than I'd ever seen her. "He's been talking off and on about Tahiti for years. What a wonderfully beautiful place for him to rest."

"When will you tell him?"

Her face glowed with anticipation. "I must plan a very special way to present the tickets to him." She gushed about the luxurious anniversary gifts he'd presented to her other years. Everything from cashmere sweaters to diamond bracelets. You would have thought, listening to her talk, that material things ranked highest on her list of important things in life. I wondered where simple words or deeds of kindness and affection ranked.

By the time the dessert tray came around, I had decided I never wanted to be rich, and I was anxious to leave. The black-coated waiter held the gleaming silver tray with a variety of delicacies for us to choose from. His accent was French or Italian, I wasn't sure which. For Saundra, it was chocolate mousse, slightly chilled; for me, the simplest dessert I could find: strawberry cheesecake.

We arrived home long before Tyler, and I rushed downstairs to Andie's room, expecting to find her up and reading in bed. The big surprise was that her bed was made and her room picked up.

"Andie," I called, even searching outside on her private balcony. "We're back!"

I checked her bathroom and found that she'd taken a shower. A pile of dirty clothes was left lying on the floor in the corner near the sink. Her makeup bag was unzipped, with mascara and blush shoved into it sloppily.

And then I spotted a clue to her whereabouts. Above the sink, on the flat piece of glass running across and below the mirror, I noticed a business card with the words "BEACH

BUZZ, The Band." Under the words were Rico's name and phone number.

"Oh, so she stayed home to see Rico," I muttered angrily, remembering the tired, worn-out-and-desperate-to-sleep charade she'd put on for me earlier. Talk about lies. Andie was the master of deceit!

Not sure what to do, I ran upstairs to the deck and scanned the beach area. She was nowhere in sight.

I headed to Tyler's room and focused his telescope, aiming north toward Rico's parents' estate. No sign of Andie.

Then I looked toward the ocean, turning the black knob, bringing a rectangular white speck into view.

Bingo! There she was. Way, way out—past the breakers— floating on an air mattress built for two were my friend and her cohort. Quickly, I cranked the view in even closer. Shoot, I could almost reach out and touch them, which is exactly what Rico was doing to Andie. Touching her hair, caressing her face. Why was she letting him get so close?

Not only had Andie decided the first day we'd come here that Rico was husband material, but here she was acting like they were married already! Well . . . not exactly married like on a honeymoon or anything, but getting terribly close. I almost felt guilty watching the two of them carry on this way. I held my breath, scared he was going to kiss her.

Tyler came bursting into the room. "Having fun?" He came over to me. "Who're you spying on today?"

I backed up, moving away from the telescope. "I, uh, hope you don't mind."

"Go for it."

"You sure?" I inched forward, almost afraid to look again.

"Go ahead and watch them," he said, grinning. "They don't know it, but last night I caught them outside together."

Andie had been with Rico in the middle of the night?

Tyler kept talking. "Man, would my mom have a cow if I did that!"

"Of course she would," I said, trying not to overreact to the shocking news. "You have no business sneaking out of the house with a girl."

"I didn't mean *that*," he said. "I meant leaving the house in the middle of the night. You never know what's lurking around out there on the beach." He sounded for real, but I didn't know what he was talking about.

"Are there prowlers or something?"

"Drug dealers, prowlers, you name it—we've got it going on up and down the beach. And the parties. Sometimes I have to put earplugs in my ears."

Now my heart was pounding out of control. Was Rico's party going to be one of those wild ones? And if so, was Rico involved in drugs or alcohol?

I got brave right then. I asked Tyler if he'd ever seen Rico drinking. "Oh, sure. Some of his college friends come up from San Diego almost every weekend. They have some rock band; I forget what it's called. All I know is there's tons of beer bottles scattered around the next morning."

I shuddered to think about Andie and her dreams of Rico being her future husband. If she only knew!

16

I shouldn't have been surprised.

Andie refused to believe me when I told her what I knew about Rico, his band, and his wild parties. I cornered her as she came into her room to shower and dress for supper.

"Holly, get a life!" she yelled. "I wouldn't think of butting into your time with Sean."

"Because nothing's happening with Sean and me."

"Right." She threw her wet towel at me. "I'm sick of your holy-schmoly routine, Holly Meredith."

"You didn't have to lie to me today," I accused her.

"I didn't lie, just changed my mind."

"What? About sleeping in? Come on! You pretended to be tired just so you could stay home."

She shook her head defiantly. "That's not how it happened, but it's really none of your business, anyway."

"Okay, fine," I said, throwing her towel down on the carpet. "But the next time your mother calls, I'm telling her the truth."

"See if I care!" She slammed her bathroom door, punctuating her words.

Jittery and upset, I went to the sitting room. Things were so far out of control. Andie couldn't even begin to see the truth about Rico. And worse, there seemed to be no way to get through to her. What could I do to make her see who Rico really was *before* she did something she might regret forever?

♥   ♥   ♥

At supper, Daddy announced that everything was set for our trip to Universal Studios.

"Cool," Tyler shouted.

"Tyler, please," Saundra reprimanded him. "We're having supper."

"Sorry," he said, but I could see his enthusiasm was oozing right out of his pores.

"What about the rest of you?" Daddy asked.

"Fine with me," Saundra said. I agreed, too.

Andie, however, looked a little nervous. "How long will we be gone?" she asked.

"Why? Got a date?" Tyler piped up.

Andie shrugged. "Just wondered."

"I thought we could have dinner somewhere special and then drive up the coast and see the sunset." Daddy pursed his lips, waiting for her response.

"Sure, sounds fine," Andie said eventually, even though I was sure Rico had told her about his beach party.

As it turned out, Andie refused to discuss her plans about Rico later that night. We'd reached a standstill, Andie and I, and to push things with her would only bring more hostility between us. So I made the decision to back off, let her do her thing, and pray for her. Mom had always said that prayer was more powerful than anything you could ever do or say.

So I prayed before going to bed, and later while trying to fall asleep. Then, first thing the next morning, and every single time I thought about Andie or began to worry over the situation.

One thing for sure, the trip to Universal Studios would keep her from Rico most of the day. That was something to be thankful for.

♥   ♥   ♥

Andie chose to hang out with Tyler on both Jurassic Park, The Ride and the E.T. Adventure. It had to be obvious to the rest of the family that Andie and I weren't speaking. I hoped it wasn't spoiling things for them, and I tried to keep a positive, upbeat attitude.

Later Saundra freaked out over the two-thousand-pound eating machine otherwise known as Jaws. When we least expected it, it leaped out of the water just inches away from her side of the tour bus.

"Oh, honey," she squealed and cuddled up to Daddy. What really got her, of course, was the water it sprayed at her while thrashing around in a frenzy to "devour" her.

King Kong was an encounter with a thirty-foot, thirty-thousand-pound, howling terror. When the hairy beast ripped the cable lines to our tram, causing a fire, a helicopter was flown in to "rescue" us. Then it was on to the earthquake, where we experienced an 8.3 heart-pounding tremor.

Out of the entire day, Daddy seemed to enjoy most the WaterWorld show. And I noticed him laughing at the tribute to *I Love Lucy*.

Of course, we scurried here and there, standing in long lines and snacking on junk food and pop while we moved from one attraction to another. One time, when Daddy and I were alone getting caramel corn, I almost told him about Andie's crush on Rico. Then, just as I was about to open my mouth and confide in him, I decided not to. I didn't want to worry him about it—and maybe cause more stress on his heart.

Later, while waiting in line for sodas, Saundra spotted a girl with waist-length hair the color of mine. Her hair had been permed in a spiral wrap and hung in gentle, vertical waves down her back. "Holly, look," she said. "Your hair would look wonderful that way."

"You think so?"

"Definitely," Andie said, the first she'd spoken to me all day.

"Really?" Now I was excited.

"If you think your mother wouldn't mind, we could have it done while you're here," Saundra suggested.

"Daddy, what do you think?" I asked.

He cocked his head, looking at me with his eyebrows raised. "It won't kink up or anything, will it?"

"It better not." I touched my single braid, not sure now how I felt about Saundra's idea.

"Then I'm all for it." He paid for the sodas and passed them down the line to Tyler, Andie, Saundra, and me.

"So, are you gonna do it?" Andie asked.

"I'm probably too chicken," I said, filing the idea away for future reference. Who knows, maybe I'd get brave and have it done right before school started. A new look would be perfect, especially to start my freshman year.

♥ ♥ ♥

"Did everyone have a good time today?" Daddy asked as we drove back down the coast at dusk after supper.

"Universal Studios was way cool." Tyler smiled up at

Saundra from the front seat, where he sat between my dad and his mom.

"Maybe we'll go again next summer," Daddy said, grinning. He turned around to glance at me in the backseat with Andie. "What do you say, Holly?"

I glanced at Andie to my left, wondering if he was including her in the invitation. "Sure, let's do it," I said.

Daddy kept talking about the events of the day while Saundra nodded off every so often. We all seemed a bit frazzled from our hectic day. All but Andie. She seemed jazzed. Probably the beach party . . . and the prospect of seeing Rico again.

That thought made me cringe, but I kept my feelings hidden, praying silently instead.

After we were home only a few minutes, Daddy got the bright idea to invite Sean over. "We'll play that Bible board game I just bought," he said, opening the built-in oak shelving unit opposite the fireplace. "Okay with you, Holly?"

What a matchmaker!

"I guess," I said, trying to hide my smile.

Saundra looked completely baffled about the new game. But she was quiet about it and didn't raise a protest.

♥   ♥   ♥

We tried our best to get Andie involved, but she wasn't interested. Daddy literally begged her to play, but she declined. "Thanks anyway," she said without an explanation. And she scurried off, down the steps, while I shot another silent prayer heavenward.

It didn't take long for Sean to show up, and after a few instructions from the manual, we began to play. I couldn't stop thinking about my beach speech to him about just being friends. And here was Daddy throwing the two of us together.

In fact, Daddy was close to winning when he got up rather abruptly and excused himself. "Sorry, kids," he said, winking at Sean. "I think I'll call it a night."

That rascal! I couldn't believe he was going to simply abandon the game like this. And Saundra was no help whatsoever. She took Daddy's arm and accompanied him down the hallway, leaving Sean and me to finish the game amidst the light of candles and soft music.

Sean seemed amused. "Look what they've done." He chuckled a little, his eyes reflecting the twinkling light of Saundra's best-smelling French vanilla candles.

"What's so funny?"

He forced the smile away. "Oh, nothing." He said it with a silly straight face now.

"Uh-huh," I said under my breath.

"What's *that* supposed to mean?" he asked, not able to hold back his grin.

His gaze was downright attentive. And, I didn't understand it, but I felt giddy. Inside and out. Shoot, my hands were damp, and I wasn't sure, but it seemed like my heart was racing out of control. Why was this happening? Sean was just a friend, wasn't he?

"Holly," he started to say.

"No, please, let's just finish the game, okay?" My eyes stared down at the board between us.

He reached over and covered my hand with his. "I can't lie to you anymore, Holly." His voice was unbearably sweet.

I felt his gaze on me and couldn't resist. My eyes found his. "About what?" I whispered.

"About your friendship notion." He took a deep breath, like this wasn't the easiest thing in the world to be saying. "I guess I just can't go along with it. I like you as a friend, but . . ." He was searching for words. "But, I want you to think about something."

He was positively adorable, sitting here across from me in my father's living room. What was he thinking, spoiling our evening like this?

I withdrew my hand. "So you're saying you didn't really agree with me before? That you were just going along with me that day on the beach? That you—"

"Holly, I think you're special. I want you to be my girlfriend." He spoke with purpose. "Those were little white lies I told you on Wednesday. I'm sorry."

This wonderful person had just asked me to change my mind. To break my promise to myself. And yet the gentle, kind way he approached the subject told me he was sincere. A true friend.

"I . . . I don't know, Sean. What I said is really important to me," I replied, referring to my earlier decision.

"*You're* important to me," he said.

Silence settled in around us as the candles flickered and the distant sounds of a rock band found its way to my ears. Thoughts of Andie clouded my thinking, and I searched for the perfect words.

Sean smiled thoughtfully. "Will you please think about it?"

Thank goodness. At least I wouldn't have to decide anything tonight.

I did myself a favor and didn't check on Andie before I went to bed, even though I was very curious. I figured what I didn't know wouldn't hurt as much. Besides, if she'd gone to meet Rico, there was only one thing I could do, down on my knees!

In my prayer, I didn't want to include a P.S. to God about Sean Hamilton, though. I was torn between feeling betrayed and knowing inside that Sean was probably the best thing that had ever happened to me.

He certainly wasn't an immature, obnoxious flirt like Jared Wilkins. And I couldn't imagine him ever acting spoiled or using Scripture to get his own way like Danny Myers.

There was one problem, though. A thousand miles separated Sean's home from mine. Long-distance romances were for the birds, and once I got back to Dressel Hills this fact would hit me for sure. I didn't have to pray about something so foolish. Sean Hamilton, like it or not, would just have to stick with my original decision.

I was starting to doze off when I thought of Andie again. What if she *hadn't* gone out to the beach with Rico? What if she was actually sound asleep in her room?

Tired but inquisitive, I hurried to check. The moonlight played on the floor near her bed and for a minute, I thought she was curled up there in her white caftan. Maybe praying?

A closer look told the truth. Andie was not in her room as I'd hoped. Now I wished I'd stayed in bed. Troubled, I pulled back her covers and lay down, resting my head on her pillow. I stared at the lighthouse painting on the wall across the room.

"Dear Lord," I whispered into the darkness, "I can't handle this thing with Andie. It's just too heavy."

My tears rolled onto her pillow. "Please watch over my friend, wherever she is right now. If she's in trouble, will you help her? I'm glad you always stay awake and never have to sleep, because I'm too exhausted to wait up all night, even though I wish I could. Good night, Lord, and thanks. Amen."

A peace settled over me, and I fell asleep in Andie's bed.

♥   ♥   ♥

The next morning when I awakened, I looked around. No sign of Andie. Then, going to my room, I found her snuggled down in my bed, mouth hanging open in a perfectly relaxed state. *Okay,* I thought, relieved. *She's back, safe and sound.*

After a quick shower, I had breakfast with Daddy and Saundra while Andie and Tyler slept in. Daddy seemed to be in a big hurry to leave for the office.

"It's Saturday, Daddy. Can't you stay home?" I pleaded.

"Someone's got to work," he said, reminding me that he'd taken off yesterday.

"What's wrong with two days off in a row?" I asked.

"All play and no work makes for a lousy retirement," he

teased. When he finished his granola and grapefruit, Daddy made a beeline down the hall.

Saundra shook her head. "What will it take to slow that man down?"

"Well, it looks like you can't make him, and I sure can't. . . ." I buttered my toast, wondering what those lab tests had shown. Surely they weren't anything to worry about, or else Daddy's doctor would have ordered bed rest or something else drastic.

Saundra began to clear the table while I was still eating, but suddenly she sat down. "Have you given that perm any more thought?" she asked.

"A little." I reached for the strawberry jam.

"Well, I have plenty of time today. If you'd like, I could drive you over to Marcie's. Afterward, we could pick up some sandwiches and have a picnic on the beach."

I twirled the perm thing around in my brain. If it turned out fabulous like the girl at Universal Studios, I'd be going home looking like a zillion bucks. "Let me think about it some more, okay?"

"Oh, sure," Saundra said. "We've got all next week."

Daddy hustled through the kitchen carrying his black leather briefcase. I hurried to catch up with him. "Wait a minute," I called. He turned around and let me kiss him good-bye. "I love you," I said. "Hurry home."

"You're a darling girl, Holly. I'll see you tonight."

A few minutes later, Tyler clumped into the kitchen looking like something the cat dragged in. "What's for breakfast?" he asked, his auburn hair sticking out all over.

"You're a little late, dear," Saundra said. "But . . . what would you like?"

He pulled out a chair and fell into it with a thud. "I could go for some waffles," he said, yawning.

Saundra had just cleaned up her now-spotless kitchen and put everything away, and here was Tyler requesting a full-blown breakfast. I wondered how his mom would react to the request.

"Waffles or French toast, dear?" she asked.

His reply was, "Waffles, with a side of scrambled eggs."

This was so unbelievable. Saundra instantly set to work creating a made-to-order breakfast. She glanced at me from the counter where she was measuring the waffle mix. "What about Andie? Do you think she'd like something to eat?"

"I'll check." I dashed to the stairs to see if Andie was still in her former zombie state.

When I got downstairs, I looked for Andie in my room. She'd already made my bed and picked up her clothes. I figured she was back in her own room, so I hurried to the door and knocked. "Andie, you up?"

"Come in," she said. Her voice sounded muddled, like she'd been crying.

I went in and closed the door behind me. "Are you okay?"

She sat on her unmade bed, her arms crisscrossed in front of her. "Not really." She sighed. "It's just . . ." Her voice trailed off.

"What's wrong?" I sat at the foot of the huge bed, facing her. That's when I noticed she was trembling.

She pulled the covers around her. "Oh, Holly."

I rushed to her side.

She could hardly talk for the tears. "It's . . . it's Rico. And . . . you were right."

"Shh," I said, stroking her back. "Just relax." But deep inside I was starting to suspect what I might be right about.

"Rico . . . uh, we . . ." She coughed, still crying. "I went to his beach party last night. After his band played awhile, he said he wanted to talk to me. Somewhere private."

Yikes, such bad news.

I tried to listen, eager to help her through whatever seemed to be upsetting her. "What happened?"

She sniffled and reached for a tissue. "We were walking down the beach, holding hands, when he started kissing me."

"You actually let him?"

She nodded slowly, watching me, testing to see if I was going to totally freak out or keep listening. I opted to listen because it was obvious Andie needed a friend.

She started talking again. "His breath smelled like beer. I pulled away, but he wanted me to sit on the beach with him."

"What did you do?"

"His speech was slurred. I should've known better than to be alone with him."

"You're saying he was drunk? Oh, Andie."

She nodded. "I was so scared. I pushed him away and said that you were expecting me here. Then I ran home as fast as I could."

"Let me get you more tissues," I said, worried sick about her.

Andie blew her nose, taking deep breaths. "You knew all along, Holly. Rico was no good." She shivered.

I put my arm around her, and she leaned her head on my shoulder. "You okay?"

"Uh-huh," she whispered. "Nothing worse happened."

"Thank goodness," I said, realizing how risky the whole situation had been. "I was praying for you late last night."

"In my bed?" She blinked her big brown eyes, smiling. "You're a wonderful friend, Holly, and I promise I won't make you cover for me ever again."

"That's good, because I was running out of lies. Actually, I hated the deceit," I confessed. "And I wish I had confided in your mom about all this."

She nodded. "I know how you must've felt, Holly. It was *my* fault you didn't. . . . I made you promise, remember?" She flung her arms around me.

After a quiet moment, I began to pray. "Dear Lord, thanks so much for protecting Andie. Forgive us both for our faithless words, and help us remember this very hard lesson. Amen."

After the prayer, I tried not to think what might've happened to her out there—if God hadn't answered my prayers.

"I'm just glad you're okay."

"You're not the only one," she said, smiling through her tears.

I heard Saundra calling, announcing brunch.

"Oh, I almost forgot. Do you want some waffles?"

"Sounds good." She hopped off the bed. Together we went upstairs, my friend and I, both equally thankful for the end of the Rico nightmare.

18

Andie was pouring syrup over her second waffle when the phone rang. Tyler leaped out of his chair, fully awake now, and grabbed the phone. When he'd said "Hello," he listened for a moment, then said, "For you, Mom."

"I wonder who that could be," Saundra said, making her way across the spacious kitchen.

I sat at the table, watching Tyler and Andie chow down, tuning out Saundra's conversation. But suddenly I realized her voice sounded strained. Really tense. And when I looked at her, I noticed that her face had turned chalk white.

She was clutching the phone with both hands. "Yes, yes . . . oh, dear, this can't be. I'll come right away. Yes, I'll meet you there."

Hands trembling, Saundra hung up the phone. "Your father collapsed at work," she told me. "He's being rushed to the hospital."

I gasped. "Is it his heart?"

Tyler held his fork in midair, staring up at his mother.

She said no more but headed down the hallway. I followed at her heels, right into her Victorian bedroom. "I want to go with you, Saundra," I stated.

"I need you to stay with Tyler, dear."

"What about Andie? Let *her* stay with him."

She shook her head. "No, no, it'll work out much better if you're here." And she literally shooed me out of her way.

"Please don't do this," I cried outside her door. "Please, Saundra, he's my father."

My emotions went crazy—anger and terror mixed together. Anger at Saundra for shutting me out, and absolute, total fright for Daddy and his condition.

How could she do this? How could she make me stay home while Daddy was probably having a heart attack . . . possibly dying. What a wicked stepmother!

I sobbed, replaying his words to me this morning. *You're a darling girl, Holly . . . I'll see you tonight.* What if those were his last words to me? What if I never saw Daddy alive again?

I choked back the tears. Back in the kitchen, Tyler was staring at his half-empty plate. "Somebody better pray," he said, sniffling.

"Let's go into the living room," I said, leading the way. Tyler and Andie followed. It was Andie who offered to pray for Daddy, and I knew she did it out of love for me. Her prayer was a powerful one, and it took some of the sting away.

Just as she said "Amen," Saundra flew through the house, grabbing up a sweater from the closet in the entryway. "I'll call you as soon as I know something."

"The second you know?" I pleaded.

"Yes, dear," she said.

So, I had Saundra's word on it. Not nearly as good as being there myself, but it would have to do. Saundra was stubborn sometimes, and since I was a guest in her house, I couldn't actually throw a fit about it, could I?

The three of us stood in front of the window watching Saundra's white sports car back out of the driveway. I glanced down at Tyler. Big tears rolled down his cheeks. "I hope Daddy doesn't die," he sobbed. "He's the only real father I ever had."

Kneeling down, I threw my arms around him and drew him near. "I know," I said, trying to swallow the huge lump in my throat. "I know."

It seemed important for me to be strong for him, letting his fears, and his tears, pour onto my shoulder.

Conscious of the passage of time, I felt the air going in and out of my nose, the pounding of my pulse—I was aware of Tyler's little body heaving against mine. And of something else.

Andie. She wrapped her arms around both Tyler and me. It was the dearest thing she could've done.

When the phone rang, I was the first to break up our huddle. I dashed to the kitchen. "Hello?"

"Holly, I just heard the news." It was Sean. "My older brother works with your dad. He just called. Are you all right?"

I couldn't speak. Hearing Sean talk about Daddy and what had just happened made me want to cry.

"Holly?"

"It's just . . . so . . . ."

"I'm praying," he said in a whisper. "We all are."

I didn't know who "we" meant, but I figured his family was. "Thanks," I squeaked out.

"Anything I can do?" he asked gently.

"Yes . . . there is. Can you hold on a second?"

I covered the phone and called to Tyler, "Will your mom freak out if I show up at the hospital after all?"

"She'll get over it," he said. "She wasn't thinking clearly, that's all."

"You're sure?"

Andie piped up. "You go, Holly. I'll stay here with Tyler." Her eyes were serious, almost sad.

I turned back toward the phone. "Sean? I was wondering, would you mind driving me to see my dad? At the hospital?"

"I'll be right over. Fifteen minutes, max."

"Thanks." He said good-bye, and I hung up.

I leaned against the kitchen wall, hoping and praying Daddy was going to be all right. Then, remembering what Saundra had said about Daddy's prayer list, I felt compelled to locate his Bible. Hurrying to their room, I found it lying on the lamp table beside the bed.

Reverently, I turned to the back pages. There, I found his prayer list. Tears clouded my vision and I struggled to see through the blur. Saundra's name was number one!

I thought of the many years I'd prayed for Daddy's salvation. And God had answered. Now, Daddy's desire was to see his wife come to know Jesus, too.

I decided to leave his Bible here at home where it belonged . . . where *he* belonged.

♥   ♥   ♥

When Sean arrived, he came to the front door and rang the bell. He was wearing beige khakis and a light blue shirt. His warm smile comforted me.

Sean waited for me to say good-bye to Tyler and Andie. "I'll call the minute I know something," I promised.

Tyler stood on tiptoes and kissed my cheek. "Tell Dad I'm praying for him."

Thrilled to hear these words, I hugged my stepbrother. "You better believe I will."

Outside, Sean opened the passenger door for me, then hurried around to get in on the driver's side. We rode in silence most of the way.

Later, looking concerned, he asked if Saundra had told me about Daddy's condition.

"Apparently he had a small attack about two years ago. She didn't say much more."

He nodded. "How did Saundra take the news about your dad . . . today?"

"Frazzled, like she didn't know what to do first," I said, remembering how she'd hurried to her bedroom and then out to the closet to get her sweater and purse. "She's probably in denial."

"We need to pray for her," he said quietly.

"Sometimes things like this pull people toward Christ," I said, remembering how Daddy had reacted to his sister's death eighteen months ago.

"And your dad has several prayer partners who are remembering Saundra right now."

I looked over at him. "Are you one of them?"

His face lit up. "As a matter of fact, I am."

"I have to be honest with you," I said hesitantly. "When I first met Saundra, I couldn't stand her. She really bugged me. Everything at the house—her clothes, the way she talked—had to be perfect. But since then, I've discovered another side to her. She's so caring. Shoot, she'd give you the shoes off her feet, I think. Not that she doesn't already have a zillion pairs."

He laughed at that.

"You know what I mean," I said.

We went for several miles without talking. But the closer we got to the hospital, the more I realized the seriousness of Daddy's situation.

Childhood memories began to flood back. Especially the times when Carrie and I were little. Daddy would read to us on Sunday afternoons. We'd snuggle into a big comfortable chair together in his upstairs study while he read the old classics aloud. Books like *Peter Pan* and *The Secret Garden*. To our delight, he would change his voice to match each character.

And there were those still, magical nights in deep summer when Daddy and I sang in harmony on the porch swing late into the night. Dear memories, never to be forgotten.

How I loved my father. I loved him in spite of his leaving us. In spite of the divorce.

Quickly, I reached for my purse and pulled out a tissue, staring out my window. But Sean had seen the tears, and against my will my eyes filled to the brim.

"Hey, are you okay?" he asked tenderly.

I tried to reassure him, forcing a weak smile. "It's so scary to think that Daddy might . . ."

Sean reached over and took my hand, not saying more. His hand enveloped mine, and despite the fact that he'd asked me to be his girlfriend last night, I knew this gesture was meant to be purely comforting, nothing more.

We rode in silence as I composed myself, and a short time later the hospital came into view. Sean found a parking spot close to the main entrance. Inside, he asked for directions to the cardiac unit, and after a quick elevator ride, we arrived on the fourth floor. The smell of antiseptic was strong as the elevator door opened. I hated the thought of Daddy being here.

I told the nurse behind the counter who I was. "My father is Robert Meredith."

Without blinking an eye, she said, "Come right this way." We followed her to a private waiting area around the corner and down the hall.

Saundra looked up with a tearstained face. "Oh, Holly . . ." She stood up and rushed over. "I'm so glad you're here." Spying Sean, she thanked him for bringing me. "I'm sorry I left you at home that way," she said, still holding my hands. "It was just such a frightening time, I—"

"I understand."

Sean slipped out to the hall, giving us privacy. I let Saundra hug me, and I cried in her arms. "How's Daddy?" I finally blurted out.

She held on to my hands as we sat down. "The doctors are with him now." She glanced up at a TV monitor high on the wall. "That's your father's room."

The heart monitor continued its monotonous beeping—a good sign. "Daddy's heart?"

She nodded. "I doubt that he'd be overjoyed about being televised like this."

I cracked a smile briefly. "Are they going to do bypass surgery?"

She seemed hesitant to respond. "Two of his arteries are ninety percent blocked. And from what the cardiologist says, they're trying a clot-busting drug on him first." She sighed audibly. "If that doesn't work, they may consider angioplasty."

I was afraid to ask. All of it sounded hideous.

Saundra seemed to understand my reluctance to inquire. She let go of my hands and used her own to demonstrate the surgical procedure. "Angioplasty is used to open a coronary artery. A small balloon is inserted into the blood vessel, compressing the plaque against the wall of the artery."

I tried not to visualize what she was describing, maybe because she kept using the word *blood* as in blood vessel and blood work.

Frightened and worried, I went back into the hall to find Sean. "It's okay for you to come in," I told him.

He frowned. "Are you sure?"

"You don't have to leave, do you?" I asked. The truth was I didn't want him to go just yet.

"Not really," he replied. "If Saundra stays the night, I'll be happy to drive you home." He was so eager to help.

The three of us flipped through magazines and talked occasionally, waiting for the doctors' decision. After another hour passed, I was beginning to wonder if something had gone wrong. Why was it taking so long?

Finally several doctors came into the private waiting area. I held my breath, wishing with all my heart this day might have a happy ending.

19

All the doctor talk of blood and balloons—and that horrible hospital smell—had made me queasy. Quickly, I left for the rest room while the doctors informed Saundra of the results of Daddy's EKG and lab work.

Inside the ladies' room, I splashed cold water on my face. Leaning over the sink, I closed my eyes. "Dear Lord," I prayed, "I've learned not to hold on when it's much better to let go and completely trust you for things like this. I really can't do this hospital scene . . . I'm really scared for Daddy. And for me. Please help the doctors and Saundra know what to do to help. Amen."

When I finally got it together and returned to the waiting room, Saundra and Sean were nowhere to be seen. One of the nurses came in and said Sean had headed back to the beach house to get Tyler and Andie. "Your stepmother is in the prayer chapel just down the hall." She touched my arm, guiding me in the right direction.

I hurried to the chapel door. Holding my breath, I inched the door open and saw Saundra kneeling at the altar. A large crucifix hung on the wall above her. I tiptoed into the peaceful place, making my way soundlessly toward the altar to Saundra.

She turned slightly as I knelt close beside her.

"This is all so strange to me," she whispered, glancing up at the form of Christ on the cross.

I listened intently.

"I guess I've been wondering about God all my life," she explained, "but I was never truly able to bring myself to believe in a personal Being. But just now, as I was praying, I found myself talking to Him as though He were someone real, someone who cares about what happens to your father."

I wiped the tears from my eyes and found it curious that she simply let hers drip off her face. Searching in the chapel, I found a box of tissues on a chair beside the wall. I offered her one.

"Thanks, Holly," she said, without the *dear*. It was comforting to hear my name without her automatic tag.

She spoke of their first meeting—hers and Daddy's—with fondness, and even though I always thought I'd resist hearing this story, I found myself eager to listen. "Your father was floundering emotionally when I first met him. We happened to be attending the same support group. He was almost shy, definitely reserved. Desperately lonely."

Lonely for us? For the family he'd left behind?

She continued. "After several sessions, your father found enough confidence to share his story with the group. Such a sad, despairing tale. He told how he'd abandoned his family, how he'd been selfish and self-centered, how he'd hurt his wife and children. My heart went out to him." She paused, taking a deep breath. "You see, Holly, I'd been hurt desperately, as well, only not in a similar way. . . ." She didn't reveal the reason for her divorce, but it seemed that her former husband had done the leaving—two weeks before Christmas, no less!

I touched her arm. "You helped Daddy through his pain, didn't you?"

She nodded. "We helped each other. Now we must do

the same," she said, her head down. "If Christ can make himself real to your father, stubborn and strong-willed as he is, maybe there's something to all this God business."

I wanted to help. "Sometimes it's hard to trust," I said. "But if you ask the Lord to become real to you, I know He will." I put my arm around her. "I believe something else, too."

She began to cry again.

"I believe Daddy is in very good hands." By the tentative smile on her glistening face, I knew she understood.

Much later, the surgeon, still wearing his green scrubs, met all of us in the waiting room. "Robert is stabilized and in very good condition. He held up well during the angioplasty, and we'll know better tomorrow how things stand after we do a follow-up EKG and some lab work." His serious face broke into a wide smile. "Things look very good at the present time."

Tyler stood up. "Will my dad be able to go Boogie boarding with me again?"

"That's certainly a good possibility," the surgeon said, chuckling.

"So you're saying he's going to be fine?" I asked, while Andie draped her arm around my shoulders.

The surgeon nodded.

I heard Saundra whisper, "Thanks, God."

♥   ♥   ♥

Later Sean brought sacks filled with hamburgers and fries—definitely not appropriate food for the cardiac patients in the units surrounding our little waiting room. But the emotional day had depleted all of us, so we were thankful for Sean's gracious gesture.

"Here, let me reimburse you," Saundra said, opening her purse and pulling out a wad of bills.

Sean put up his hands. "The treat's on me."

Just then the head nurse came in and told us we could see Daddy. Each of us would have three minutes with him. Saundra first, then me, then Tyler. Only one family member could be in the room at any given time.

We were all so anxious to see him, crossing our fingers about the procedure. If his arteries stayed open, they'd have him up walking soon, and later doing the treadmill thing. Maybe, just maybe, Daddy would get to come home on Wednesday. If so, we'd have him all to ourselves for five whole days before Andie and I were scheduled to leave for home.

While I waited my turn, Sean and I went for a short walk down the hall to the sun-room. It was still light out, and the ferns and plants scattered around made the room pleasant and airy.

"I guess we need to talk," I said as we sat near one of the windows.

Sean smiled, which made his eyes twinkle. "Good news, I hope."

"Well, yes . . . and no."

He looked puzzled.

I continued, "Well, yes, we should continue being good friends, and no, I can't go out with you . . . at least, not yet." I explained that my mom had always said I should be at least fifteen before I actually dated anyone. And then, only in a group.

"I'll wait," he said calmly. "You're worth waiting for, Holly."

I swallowed. "Are you for real? You mean you're not going to try and change my mind?"

"Why should I?" His eyes studied mine. "Friendship is one of the highest forms of love."

Who'd said anything about love?

"Okay, it's settled, then," I said, feeling fabulously comfortable with this guy. "When I get back home, I'll send you some letters."

"Probably not as often as *I* will."

"We'll see," I said, grinning.

Quickly, he glanced at his watch. "I think it's your turn to see your dad." We hurried down the hall, and when our hands bumped slightly, Sean didn't reach for mine. There would be plenty of time for that—with or without Sean. For now, it was great to have someone who cared but wasn't pushy. A true friend.

Standing outside Daddy's room, I leaned against the wall, feeling hopeful. Saundra and I had shared a very special moment in the chapel. I was beginning to see who she was on the inside. And Andie? Well, there was no telling how far she and I were destined to go as friends. Shoot, we'd been through a living nightmare together and survived.

Saundra came out just then, her eyes bright with joy. "He's doing wonderfully."

"Are you sure?" I whispered, glancing around the corner at Daddy all wired up with monitors and IVs and things.

"Don't worry," she reassured me. "He's fine. Go give him a kiss."

"Okay." I tiptoed into Daddy's room and stood beside his bed. Touching his hand, I whispered, "Daddy?"

His eyes fluttered open. "Holly-Heart," he said. "You're here."

I leaned over and kissed his forehead.

"Guess your old man better slow down a little, eh?"

"For starters," I said. "We want you around for a very long time."

He squeezed my hand. "Oh, I'm not going anywhere."

"Promise?"

Solemnly, he nodded. "I promise."

I couldn't help it—a tiny giggle escaped my lips. What a fabulous day this had turned out to be.

♥   ♥   ♥

Sean showed up on Sunday. We sang a few hymns softly for Daddy, and when we came to "Amazing Grace," Saundra joined in. Later, she and I took turns reading to him from his Bible.

Daddy, being a highly motivated fellow, couldn't be kept in bed for long. By Monday morning he was up walking the halls and phoning Carrie long distance. On Tuesday, he passed his first treadmill test and was moved to a regular floor. Wednesday, after lunch, we brought Daddy home. He was discharged to a cardiac rehab clinic nearby, where he'd have to check in for therapy.

Andie and I took turns helping Saundra cook his fat-free diet. Tyler played waiter, serving him breakfast on the deck, picnics on the beach, and supper by candlelight in the dining room. Andie and I played Daddy's Bible board game and beat him three times in a row.

Sunday evening, Saundra pulled a trick on him and hid her newly written prayer list in his napkin. "What's this?" he remarked, holding it up as he sat at the head of the elegant table.

I giggled. "What's it look like?"

Saundra beamed, coming around and hugging him. "Read it, darling."

"It's a list," he said, frowning at first. "A *prayer* list?" He read it silently first, then out loud.

"Number one, Robert's complete recovery. Number two, many more anniversaries together. Number three, a surprise trip to Tahiti with my husband. Happy anniversary!"

Tyler, Andie, and I applauded the success of her secret mission and Daddy's steady recovery.

♥　♥　♥

When I called home to Dressel Hills later that night, Mom asked if Andie was around. "She's right here, why?"

"Stan has something to say to her."

"Okay," I said cautiously as I handed her the phone.

"Hello?" she said hesitantly.

A short pause followed.

Then she said, "You're not friends with Ryan anymore? Why, what happened?"

I held my breath.

"Yeah, I know what you mean," Andie said.

Another pause. I wondered what was going on between the two of them.

Soon, Andie's grin gave her away. "Sure, I forgive you. Just don't let it happen again."

Perfect! My best friend and my brousin (cousin-turned-stepbrother) had made up. As for the Ryan Davises and the Rico Hernandezes of the world—well, prayer changes things. And people, too.

I must never forget.

The Absolute Truth:
How Honest Are You?
A Quiz

Holly grabbed her beach towel and sun block. "Little white lies aren't really white, you know," she said to Andie.

"And not so little, either," Andie said, carrying a Thermos of lemonade and her beach bag. The two girls headed across the park to the Dressel Hills Portal Pool.

"Some kids lie all the time and think nothing of it," Holly remarked. "But the problem with lying is remembering what you said."

"Yeah, so you have to tell another one to cover up the *first* lie," Andie agreed.

Holly sighed. "When it comes right down to it, the best thing is to tell the truth, even if you're in trouble, and just deal with the consequences."

Andie giggled.

"What's so funny?" Holly asked.

"I was just thinking of Danny Myers. He'd be quoting Scriptures by now."

Holly nodded. "Like the one in Proverbs. 'Truthful lips endure forever, but a lying tongue lasts only a moment.' "

"Actually I was thinking about the verse in Revelation where it talks about liars being cast into the lake of fire," Andie said. Both girls shivered.

"After what happened this summer," Holly said, "I think I'd rather go with 'truthful lips.' "

Andie agreed wholeheartedly.

So, what about you? Does the temptation to lie give you the creeps, or is it no big deal? Let's see how honest you really are. Take the honesty quiz and find out.

1. You and your friends drop in on the nearest fast-food place. Instead of change for a five, the clerk gives you change for a ten. What's your response?

   a. Keep the extra money. (Who knows how many times you've been shortchanged before. This'll balance things out, right?)
   b. Give the extra money back.
   c. Donate the extra money to your favorite charity.

2. A new family moves into your apartment complex. They need an experienced baby-sitter, at least fifteen years old. You're experienced but only fourteen. You really need the bucks. What do you do?

   a. Wear your hair up during the interview and fib if they ask your age. (After all, you look sixteen.)
   b. Volunteer your actual age in hopes of impressing them with your responsibility and honesty.
   c. Tell the truth, but only if they ask.
   d. Don't bother to interview.

3. You're grounded for the weekend—no phone calls allowed. On Saturday, Mom and Dad go out for the evening. You're bored and dying to call your best friend. What do you do?

   a. Call her. After all, you have homework questions.
   b. Surprise your mom and clean up the kitchen.
   c. Leave the house. Use the pay phone at the 7-Eleven.

4. Your friend loves her new hairstyle. But you liked it better the old way. When she asks your opinion, you say:

   a. "Looks cool."
   b. "It's okay, but I prefer the old way."
   c. "What are you doing for spring break?" (Change the subject—fast!)
   d. "Are you serious? Please, change it back!"

5. During a test, you can see the smartest kid's answers one desk away. The teacher leaves the room. You need a good grade to stay on the girls' volleyball team. So you:

   a. Sneak a peek. (The team needs you!)
   b. Rely on last night's cramming efforts.
   c. Finish the test quickly, in time to double-check the smart kid's answers. (It's not really cheating, is it?)

6. Your best friend asks you to keep a major secret. She emphasizes that you're the only one who knows. Another friend wants to hear the full scoop, too, and promises to keep it quiet. What will you do?

   a. Tell her, but make her promise not to tell.
   b. Keep the secret. You're loyal, aren't you?
   c. Tell her and five others. Your friend will understand.

7. At the amusement park, the Big Bad Wolf roller coaster entices you, but the lines are incredibly long. (A sign says there's a sixty-minute wait.) Your impatient friends begin cutting through to the front, telling people, "Mom and Dad are waiting just ahead." What do you do?

   a. Save some precious ride time and go along with the story.

   b. Wait at the end of the line ... despite what your friends do.

   c. Let your friends cut through the line, then tell people, "My pals are waiting for me just ahead."

8. Five of your friends are headed for the mall. You want to go, but your mom's not crazy about the idea. What do you tell her?

   a. "All my friends have permission." (Well, maybe three.)

   b. "You can trust me, Mom. You won't be sorry you let me go. You'll see."

   c. "They'll kick me out of the group forever if I don't go."

   d. "Please, Mom? I'll do all the dishes for a year."

9. After school, while your teacher is out of the room, you accidentally break her glass paperweight. No one sees it happen. You:

   a. Say nothing unless she asks about it.

   b. Apologize and offer to pay for the paperweight.

   c. Deny breaking it if asked.

10. Walking along the beach, you find a wallet containing $500. There's no ID, only a name inside. What do you do?

    a. Hit the nearest mega-mall and shop till you drop.

    b. Exhaust every possible lead until you find the owner.

c. Attempt to find the owner. Keep the money if you fail.

Scoring:

Give yourself two points for each "b" answer, one point for each "d" answer, and zip for each "a" or "c" answer. Subtract one point for each time you answered "b" only because you knew it was the correct response, not because that's what you'd actually do. Be honest.

20 points: Hey, you're "perfectly fabulous stuff." It appears that you take God's Word seriously and are growing stronger in your faith. Great job.

16–19 points: For the most part, you're tops on truthfulness, not to mention a girl who can be trusted. Work on the rough edges and keep trying.

10–15 points: Oops! You're in desperate need of some truth training. Crack open your Bible and take a hard look at Ephesians 4 and 5.

0–9 points: Talk to Jesus about your untruthful tendencies. Ask Him to help you be a girl of honesty and integrity. Once you get on the right track, retake the test (you ought to see a major improvement).

♥ ♥ ♥

Don't miss HOLLY'S HEART #11,
Freshman Frenzy
Available May 2003!

When Holly begins ninth grade in the high school, she's not sure she can survive the initiations. But her best friend, Andie, adjusts quickly and begins a campaign for class president—leaving Holly behind, until Holly realizes that relief can come in the most unexpected places.

About the Author

Beverly Lewis recalls the havoc one little white lie can create. "In God's eyes, there is no difference between a little white lie and a great big black one," she says. Living a life of honesty and integrity is precisely what Jesus calls us to do— it's what sets us apart as Christians in a deceitful world.

Beverly is the author of the GIRLS ONLY series, as well as the SUMMERHILL SECRETS series. "If you like Holly Meredith," she says with a grin, "you'll also enjoy Merry Hanson, Livvy Hudson, Jenna Song, Heather Bock, and Manda Garcia." See for yourself!

You can write to Beverly at *www.BeverlyLewis.com*.

Also by Beverly Lewis

PICTURE BOOKS

Cows in the House   Annika's Secret Wish
Just Like Mama

THE CUL-DE-SAC KIDS
Children's Fiction

The Double Dabble Surprise   Tarantula Toes
The Chicken Pox Panic   Green Gravy
The Crazy Christmas Angel Mystery   Backyard Bandit Mystery
No Grown-ups Allowed   Tree House Trouble
Frog Power   The Creepy Sleep-Over
The Mystery of Case D. Luc   The Great TV Turn-Off
The Stinky Sneakers Mystery   Piggy Party
Pickle Pizza   The Granny Game
Mailbox Mania   Mystery Mutt
The Mudhole Mystery   Big Bad Beans
Fiddlesticks   The Upside-Down Day
The Crabby Cat Caper   The Midnight Mystery

ABRAM'S DAUGHTERS
Adult Fiction

The Covenant

THE HERITAGE OF LANCASTER COUNTY
Adult Fiction

The Shunning   The Confession
The Reckoning

OTHER ADULT FICTION

The Postcard

The Crossroad

The Redemption of Sarah Cain

October Song

Sanctuary*

The Sunroom

www.BeverlyLewis.com

*with David Lewis